Be the Ball

Be the Ball

An Academic Inquiry Into
Synergistic Character Modalities in
Caddyshack
&
Back Nine Bushwood Paradigms

By Jeff Nelligan

Thesis Dissertation Submitted to the
Faculty of the Graduate School of Faber College
in partial fulfillment of the requirements for the degree of
DOCTOR OF PHILOSOPHY in Cinematic Sociology

April 1, 2020
New York, New York
Faculty Review Committee Members
Professor Eric Stratton, Thesis Sponsor;
Emile Faber Professor of Sociology & Academic Advisor,
Delta Tau Chi
Professor Douglas Neidemeyer, Professor of Psychology & Proctor
Emeritus, ROTC Affairs
Dr. Kent Dorfman, Director, Center for Pathologies
Dr. Vernon Wermer, President, Faber College & Chair,
Constitutional Codicil Committee

ISBN: 9798691875137

TABLE OF CONTENTS

Abstract · vii

Thesis Methodology ·ix

Doctoral Discussion· ·xi

Chapter I   Danny Noonan · · · · · · · · · · · · · · · · · · · 1
                 *Discursive Socioeconomic Reflections on "College
                 Fund" Mythologies*

Chapter II   Ty Webb · 15
                 *Gentry Radicalism: The 'Pool or Pond'
                 Conundrum*

Chapter III   Al Czervik · 31
                 *The Bayesian Gambling Reflex and
                 New Capitalist Hegemonies*

Chapter IV   Spalding Smails· · · · · · · · · · · · · · · · · · 41
                 *Neo-Generational Paradigms: Getting Nothing
                 and Liking It*

Chapter V   The Belles of Bushwood· · · · · · · · · · · 49
                 *Titular Variables in Hermeneutic Feminist
                 Marginalization*

Chapter VI   Everyone Else · · · · · · · · · · · · · · · · · · 57
                The Mob in Ethno-Centric Deviant Theory

Chapter VII   Judge Elihu Smails· · · · · · · · · · · · · · · 65
                Proto-Authoritarian Totems and The Billy
                Baroo

Chapter VIII   Carl Spackler· · · · · · · · · · · · · · · · · · 77
                Pre-Hobbesian Realism: The Himalayan
                Fantasia

Chapter IX   The 19th Hole · · · · · · · · · · · · · · · · · 93
                Towards a Unifying Theme

Acknowledgements · 97
About the Author · 100

ABSTRACT

For decades, scholars have wrestled with the normative paradigms and socio-synergistic implications of the movie *Caddyshack*. Is it a triumphalist masterpiece, an unequalled cinematic *tour de force* relying on a sublime mix of drama, pathos, and wit that announces a cinematic New Enlightenment? Or is the film an utterly base form of juvenilia, a retrograde jumble of low-brow one-liners whose popularity presages an irretrievable Western cultural decline?

This Doctoral thesis, through the rigor of Critical Golf Theory, will prove the former hypothesis and provide definitive looper clarity on *Caddyshack* as the convergence of fairway modalities and metaphoric comedic cannonballs. Like those in *Animal House*.

Furthermore, we will also take a chip shot at the oft-overlooked and little understood "Goodness v. Badness" conjunctive at the heart of the Danny Noonan – Judge Smails Redemption narrative, which has proven striking in many Post-Bushwoodian dialogues.

Strictly adhering to the Faber College Thesis Requirements, the <u>Methodology</u> provides a thorough examination of micro-character development, each individual examined in his or her contextualized space. The <u>Doctoral Discussion</u> features a seminal reframe of the film's structure and provides broad strokes on where exactly this whole thing is going.

Be the ball is not just a profound and signature admonition for Judeo-Christian marginalization but an eerie, some say striking, talisman of late 20th century Existentialism, a *Smailius Czervickiam* assimilation of the Bushwood Totality into symbolic Individualism. The Whole, as it is, in One.

...the Noonan - Smails Redemption narrative, which has proven striking in many Post-Bushwoodian 19th Hole dialogues.

Ergo, the significance of this Thesis endeavor cannot be overstated; it seeks nothing less than the rightful adjustment of *Caddyshack* to the preeminence it should enjoy in the Clubhouse Library of Western Civilization. Which is nice.

THESIS METHODOLOGY

The Methodology employs close examination of the film through the discursive peep hole of its five male protagonists and three female *ingénues*. As well, it offers a passing *positivus shockitus* glance at the toxic ethnic stew of bit players. This then, is their story – men and women composed of hopes and dreams, blood, sweat, and tears. And manganese.

So powerful are these personalities, so dense is the plot that even the keenest academicians barely comprehend that *the entire movie takes place during just a few short days.* Yes, even though the combined profundity seems to span centuries.

In addition to all this dialectics mumbo-jumbo, our thesis will explore the following thematic tautologies:

a. The social construct of the so-called 'Snobs vs. the Slobs' bifurcation, relying upon the derivative superfluities of class warfare that are certainly an unexplored theme in American arts;

b. The inherent undercurrent of sexual tension: *Exampli meatballius* - a country club called "Bushwood," a female pixie surnamed "Underall," a handsome, alluring male star named "Czervik"; and,

c. Completing the trinity: Secular-religio torment featuring an apostate Bishop, Roman Catholic microaggressions, Basho, and the 12th Son of the Lama.

This triumvirate will provide a fulsome tapestry woven as tight as a Titleist and yes, may even feature a descent into a Dante-like Tenth Circle of 18th Hole nihilism. That's because this Thesis is nothing less than a unique and historic scholastic undertaking. Yes, I know I'm boldly venturing into a never-before-explored academic rough. That's because I know there are more important things than grades.

It is only with this courageous methodological focus on the bright stars and dark symbolism that we can get off the beach and peer through the prism of space to behold the true genius of *Caddyshack*. In the words of one 20th Century prophet, we've outfinesed ourselves.

DOCTORAL DISCUSSION

Among the greatest misconceptions about *Caddyshack* is that it is a movie about caddies, or a caddy shack. Or golf.

In point of fact, *Caddyshack* is a penetrating allegory about modern Existence. Its superficial depth and panoramic sweep is unmatched in modern cinema. It touches a deep, heretofore unknown nerve in the psychological Achilles heel attached to us all. Indeed, in a symbolic sense, we may never play the game again.

The inherent undercurrent of sexual tension:
Exampli meatballius - a country club called
"Bushwood," a female pixie surnamed "Underall,"
a handsome, alluring male star named "Czervik."

Our Thesis chapter sequence endeavors to illume a subliminal glimpse into 18 Holes of the Bushwoodian Cosmos through its unique characters and Himalayan proportions.

In particular, by turning a jeweler's eye on select scenes, we will leave the cramped sand traps of Illusion for the broad fairways of Reality.

Of course, only a hopeless hacker would attempt a complete review of the film in its enormous entirety; such an undertaking would necessitate the monumental scholarship equivalent to the 1st Century B.C. Septuagint Greek translation of the Old Testament, Gibbons' *The Decline and Fall of the Roman Empire* or more recently, Von Hoffenberg's archival research in Prague on *European Vacation.*

Instead, we will only review those exquisite moments full of sound and fury in order to that we may fumigate our Thesis parameters. Yes, this may leave gaps but I am well aware that my sponsor, Professor Stratton, wanted this baby chop chop.

Indubitably, what we will find in each character, as in all of us, is the yearning and groaning for meaning and a corner piece to the puzzle of mankind's metaphysical back nine. In a soliloquy echoing around the globe on the faintness of a 3rd Hole breeze, we will discover that indeed, there is a force in the universe. All you have to do to get in touch with it is stop thinking, let things happen, and yes, *Be the Ball.*

....such an undertaking would necessitate the monumental scholarship equivalent to Von Hoffenberg's archival research in Prague on *European Vacation...*

In summary, I respectfully invite the Faculty Review Committee Members to view this Thesis as one-fourth rigorous academic inquiry, one-fourth emotive journey, and one-fourth joyous celebration.

Now let's go, while we're young.

Chapter I

Discursive Socioeconomic Reflections on
"College Fund" Mythologies

"The upper classes regard the proletarian like
a horse...he must receive enough to enable
him to work."
Karl Marx, *Wages of Labor,* 1844

"How about a Fresca?"
Judge Smails

"Danny Noonan" is perhaps one of the most difficult screen roles ever envisioned. This near-fictional character must rely on a brilliant script that builds effortlessly from strength to strength, even while standing alongside four major comedic screen performers.

Nevertheless, we receive a top-notch performance from our young Cinderella - his innocence, good humor and great swing trump his lumpen proletariat roots so as to attain a materialist conquest over a pathetic cookie jar, a St. Copius scholarship he didn't get, and a Caddy scholarship revoked as he putts to Destiny on the most important hole of his life. Indeed, he is the singular catalyst for this film.

Following our Methodological scorecard, we bring a modified scramble theory to an examination of the following scenes:

Scene I – Noonan Agonistes & Winter Rules

The film's opening moments are a staggering but subtle glimpse at the squalid, grinding poverty that is almost overplayed as a wallowing parody of a poor Catholic family short on ambition and even shorter on intellect. It's a household of runny-nosed kids fighting desperately for the last of the cold cereal in the box, a slow-witted father with a clip-on bow tie and the ultimate nickel-and-dime totem: A near-empty "College Fund" stashed in a cookie jar. Can this tableau be painted in more crude and primitive strokes? Nope.

From this gritty shabbiness we transition quickly to psychological abuse. Danny is accused of being diabetic by his scornful Dad and then threatened verbally: "I'm gonna talk with Colonel Burdick about putting him on at the lumberyard." We're 2:52 minutes into the film and already the emotional tension is unyielding.

Next is Danny's escape - *literally by fire escape* - from this domestic terror as his half-witted father bellows out to no one who is listening, certainly not the nine Dickinsonian Noonan waifs or the frumpy Mrs. Noonan: "Well, he isn't gonna be a caddy all his life, is he?!"

Frantically, Danny pedals away from the tenement on his hand-me-down bike, gazing wide-eyed at stately homes.

And oh yes, just in case you missed it, there is the symbolic crossing of the railroad tracks and finally, the drive into Bushwood Country Club. This Horatio Alger-style symbolism is so trite and belabored that counterintuitively, it excels as a conjunctive motif: We are already on Danny's side, and we haven't even met Colonel Burdick.

A near-empty "College Fund" stashed in a cookie jar. Can this tableau be painted in more crude and primitive strokes? Nope.

We time travel in our cosmic golf cart and suddenly we're at the caddyshack and that pathological gambler, Lou Loomis, is lining up caddies for the upcoming foursome. "I'll take Smails if nobody wants him," volunteers Danny. Jeers of "suck up" ring in his ears, but our young caddy is intent on Making his Future.

Moments later, we are reeling from a first-hole flare-up where gambling is not allowed at Bushwood but Judge Smails has already sliced and lost a hundred bucks. And now Danny and the Judge are in the rough on the 3rd hole.

"Don't count that. I was interfered with," says the Judge Foot Wedge, furtively kicking his ball back onto the fairway. "Yes sir," replies a supplicant Danny, who then brightly suggests, "Why don't you improve your lie, sir?" "Yes, yes, winter rules. Ah yes," replies the Judge. Winter rules indeed, in the summer sunshine. [1.]

In near-Manichean foreshadowing, Danny's slide toward Darkness has begun.

Scene II - The Yacht Club & the Maggie-Lacy Axis

Hit refresh in your mind and recollect Danny's winning finish at the 35th Annual Caddy Day Tournament. Recall his sincere smile, the inspirational music, the photo his mother takes with her cheap Polaroid camera, the tremendous innocence evinced here. It all liquefies, as we shall soon see, like melted "buddor."

"Excellent round, son! Excellent round! Top notch, top notch!!" exults Judge Smails as they walk together down the fairway to the table holding the 4-inch-tall Caddy Tourney trophy. "Say, I'm having a little party at the yacht club this Sunday. I'm christening my new sloop. What are you, you doing this Sunday?"

"No plans," says a smiling Danny.

"Great! How'd you like to mow my lawn, eh?" If we could hammer home the Marxian prole theme anymore, we couldn't.

"I figure a college-bound fellow like you could use a few extra dollars. And ah, when you're finished, why don't you drop by the yacht club, hwom? Hwom? Hwom?!"

The action swiftly moves to the yacht club with Danny bouncing up to the terrace *a la* Cary Grant. He's sincere and well-meaning and we all cringe collectively in embarrassment for him.

"I guess I'm overdressed," he says wistfully to the seductress Lacy. But even the evil diva recognizes his innate goodness.

"It depends on what's in here," she replies, putting her finger on his heart. She then reads his palm, divines the stars, and moments later, he's patting her naked thigh and musing, "I want you to know that, you know, because of this, you don't have to stop seeing other people." To which the hard-bitten Lacy collapses into a paroxysm of laughter.

Unfortunately, the scene concludes with the utter destruction of the Judge's boudoir, but not before the ever-thinking Danny throws a bath gown at a charging Smails and says, "Your robe your honor."

Subtextually elucidated, it is at this precise moment that the Redemptive transition begins to churn like a golf ball in an energized ball washer.

Danny spends that evening in the caddyshack locker room following the bedroom confrontation. Maggie arrives early that morning and he tells her he's in "big trouble." She informs him that she is too. As a matter of fact she's "laiyhte." "Late for what?" Danny asks innocently.

"For not being pregnant!" she cries and soon begins to sob uncontrollably.

Ever the stand-up guy, Danny responds, "Maggeeeee.... look, look, I'm not going to let you go through this alone... whatever you decide..."

"I'm gonna have it! I've already decided!"

Instantly, Danny instantly sees Life's All. Poor, married, the College Fund now the Diaper Fund, the horizons shuttered, the dreams ended, the looming night-shift at Colonel Burdick's mysterious lumberyard. Despite this awful vision, he knows what he must do. Quite deliberately, he intones "Well, that's it then. We'll just get married." His personal integrity is met with only one of the three examples of viciousness Maggie evinces in the film: "Oh God, 'dat's all I need!" she cries back demurely.

Subtextually elucidated, it is at this precise moment that the Redemptive transition begins to churn like a golf ball in an energized ball washer.

She then claims, while in tears, "It might not be yours, OK?" To which he replies, "Maggeeeee, I know you're just making this up about the other guys so I won't have to feel guilty." Even after he repeats his offer of marriage, she lovingly yells back "Well 'danks fer nuttin'!"

Please note that this display of courage and sacrifice is so impressive as to bring that caddyshack manager and embittered bookie, Lou Loomis, to observe, "You're a good egg, Noonan," and then add compassionately, "Pick up that Kleenex."

It's when Danny bends down to pick up that Kleenex that we hear the terrifying words, "The Judge would like to see a caddy named Danny Noonan as soon as he comes in."

Scene III – Goodness, Badness & the Fresca Gambit
Hold on to your fine shammy because we are about to witness a momentous confrontation on the screen, a crescendo into conflict and then sweet resolution, powered by a script so taut it rages like fire in dry straw.

Danny enters the Judge's office to confront the Judge, who is sitting in a swivel chair, staring at a wall.

"Judge Smails, sir," he says, tucking in his shirt.

"Danny," intones the somber legalist, "I think you know why you're here so I'll do us both a courtesy and not review what happened yesterday." The good Judge bobs and weaves behind a lamp, which he then gently throws to the floor. He clasps his hands in front of him.

"My niece is the kind of girl who has a certain zz--zz-zest for living. The last thing any of us need right now is a lot of loose talk about her behavior."

"I swear I didn't tell anybody anything, sir."

"Good. Guh guh good." Smails gets up and begins pacing the room.

"You know, despite what happened, I'm still, still convinced you have many fine qualities and I...I think you can still become a gentleman someday..."

Suddenly, like Satan himself, the Judge is looming over Danny. He grasps Danny's shoulder and looks down ominously"..."if you understand and abide by the rules of decent society."

The Judge then walks to the window and looks out thoughtfully.

"Danny, Danny. There's a lot of, wellll, badness in the world today. I see it in court every day. I've sentenced boys younger than you to the gas chamber. Didn't want to do it. Felt I owed it to them." He pauses. Then continues.

"The most important decision you can make right now is what you stand for, Danny." The Judge faces off with the air of the magistrate he is and looks at Danny.

"Goodness? Or Badness?"

The world trembles. At this moment comes one of the most transformational stage scenes that underlies this Dissertation's monumental gamble.

Danny knows what he must do. The Dark Side beckons, with a lot more allure than any lumberyard. He summons up all the deceit he can muster and says with righteous insincerity, "I know I've made some mistakes in the past. I'm willing to make up for that. I wanna be good."

"Good. Good. VERY good." The Judge and Danny then exchange two of the most false smiles in American cinematic history.

The Judge pivots expertly. "You know, I know how hard it is for young people today and I want to help. Why just ask my grandson Spalding. He and I are regular pals!"

The Judge falls serious, looks expectantly at Danny, and holds out his hand.

"Are you my pal, Mr. Scholarship winner?"

Danny hesitates for longer than a moment and the whole world trembles again. "Yes sir, I'm your pal."

The Judge beams and then utters the words that have become a signature phrase in literary anthologies everywhere:

"How 'bout a Fresca?"

> "I've sentenced boys younger than you to
> the gas chamber. Didn't want to do it.
> Felt I owed it to them."

We have reached the Mt. Everest of American drama. The back and disjointed forth, the unspoken emotions, the wide sweep of relief mixed with terror, the dishonesty and mendacity. It remains a scene of such compelling ferocity that in the final test, there are many academics who cannot and do not shy away from identifying this as the most disturbing yet fascinating scene in the film. Along with other scenes.

Scene IV – The Final Round & Sonja Heine

Pedagogically speaking, please reflect on the remarkable milestones up to this point.

Danny has bonded with Ty; has won the Caddy Tournament; has had illicit relations with Maggie and heard her welcome news; has had Lacy rooting around in his palm and yet allowed her to see other guys; and, has cleverly rebounded from that fiasco to win over the Judge and secure the Caddy scholarship. [1.] We've seemingly come to the end of it all. But not as far as we know.

Danny knows, in his very own words, he's "been a jerk lately." He knows he's traveled to the Dark Side with Smails. He's witnessed and abetted the Judge to cheat on the first nine holes of a casual $40,000 game that will ultimately decide the fate of Bushwood Country Club.

He wants to be good, sure, but how to do so?

Here's how. Danny is asked by Ty to stand in for a mortally injured Al because Sonja Henie is not available. The Judge, acutely aware of Danny's skills, growls that "Ohhhh, Danny is an employee of the club. He can't work and play, particularly something eee-lee-gulll as this."

The Judge struts near Danny, twitching his face manically in intimidation.

It is here that Danny comes face-to-face in deciding upon that which the Judge himself once lectured: Goodness or Badness.

Danny pauses one last time to contemplate the enormity of what he is about to do. Al wanders by, winking uncontrollably as he whispers a sentence I'll keep in the bag for later [3.]

Danny pauses, takes off his hat. "Welllllllllll?" bites off the Judge.

Danny chooses Goodness. "I'll play." He will sub for Al.

In an uncontrolled rage, the Judge mutters, "I guess you don't want that scholarship, do you!"

"I guess I don't," says a smiling Danny, now confident in his purity, the Pupil turning on Master, as such.

And Smails' response? A sniveling, mocking, desperate "I guess I don't, I guess I don't!"

The wager has reached a level from which the weaker amongst us intuitively recoil. Some crude, irresistible force has brought is to this point and this terrifying conflict among mortals.

The golf play immediately picks up. Danny is shown confidently sending airmails, the cinematography depicts brilliant, sunlit fairways, orchestral strings luxuriously fill the air, and it's clear that the tables have turned. Judge Smails and Dr. Beeper are now in a fight for their very golfing lives. We know because we are suddenly standing on the 18th green. And one last putt for Danny.

At this precarious moment of all-square Meaning, he receives stirring encouragement from Ty: "Don't worry about this one. If you miss it, we lose."

Also at this moment of Truth, the heavy irony is that Danny knows both men, Ty and Smails, better than they know themselves.

Also at this moment of Decision, Al Czervik intrudes. "Hey Smails, double or nothin' he makes it, eighty grand."

Also at this moment of Drama, the Judge, intent on the shot, can barely bring his lips together to answer:

"Yuhhhhhhhhh... Yesssss."

Last, also at this moment of *Schadenfreude*, Danny learns that Smails is forsaking him, that the Judge never was his "pal." *Which he, Danny, knows that he should have realized from the start.* Indeed, the world trembles again.

With new resolve, Danny glances around at the entire Bushwood congregation, all assembled for the first time, a striking, breathtaking, appalling spectacle. He contemplates the shot from several angles. Which gives rise to the Judge's refrain now translated into more than 230 languages around the world: "Welllllllllll!!! We're waiting!!"

Danny putts. After a series of massive explosions a ball that was once afraid of the dark goes home [4.]. Do we acknowledge that this true life ending is trite, hackneyed, implausible, and predictable? Is it just a cheap storyline twist ending with some ridiculously illogical and witless chain of circumstances that are completely unbelievable?

No, *Caddyshack* defies this easy compartmentalization. Everything that occurs on the 18th hole fits into the Master Plan. Which brings us back to Danny. And, as though they are joined at the hip, Judge Smails.

Which gives rise to the Judge's refrain now translated into more than 230 languages around the world: "Wellllllllll!!! We're waiting!!"

Because the fact is: One of the countless triumphs in this movie is that Danny's winning putt translates into his long sought-after college tuition. That's because, as I promised earlier, this is what Al whispered: "Hey kid, if you win, I'll make it worth your while."

Forget stuffing dollar bills into a cookie jar and nights at the lumberyard. Danny's triumph is not only over Bushwood, it is over the circumstances of his family life. Because now he can afford to go to college. And not on the Caddy Scholarship, which he doesn't have anyway because it was yanked nine holes ago.

Judge Smails' consequent fall is a sidebar to the money Danny has "earned." Consider the exquisite irony of Danny the lumpen prole excelling at the sport of kings.

So long, Colonel Burdick.

Lumberyardius Summarius

Let's take this to another level: Let us fall back on superior Biblical firepower to comprehend the meaning here. Danny, not Betty, is transformed into David (yes, that David). The metaphorical slingshot he uses is a putter, the toppled Goliath is Smails, Bushwood will descend into a burnt and blasted Sodom with Carl Spackler serving as the apocalypse-driving Devil. Or, perhaps we just say 'Thank God the Redemptive narrative is consummated.' Goodness has triumphed over Badness. And I know it's difficult to understand with me talking like this.

"I want to be good," he once told the Judge long ago and faraway. Actually, just one day ago and in the Judge's office oh, about 45 yards from the 18th green. In the end, he is.

Footnotes

1. Please see the Wack-Dittie monograph on *"Algorithmic Factoring on Below Par Scores in the Bushwood Model."* Journal of Statistical Variation, Winter, 2019.

2. What gives Danny a chance at the Caddy scholarship? Why, Carl Lippbaum has tragically died at summer camp "I hear he choked on his own vomit," says Lyle graciously.

3. Consider this astonishing fact: These are the only words exchanged between Al Czervick and Danny Noonan in the entire film.

4. Standing athwart all academic and athletic jurisprudence, the author would like to respectfully disagree with the Schoolmen who categorically defend the premise that Danny was successful in his attempt. This is absurd. The scientific conclusion is that the ball could never have been physically "stuck" on the edge of the hole. But that was needed for some kind of dramatic affect. I think.

Chapter II

Gentry Radicalism: The 'Pool or Pond' Conundrum

> "...the last gasp of Romanticism, the quelling
> of its florid uprising against the vapid formal-
> ism of one strain of the Enlightenment,...a
> certain sardonic laconicism disguising itself
> in a new sanctification of the destructive in-
> stincts...where nothing remains sacred."
> Stephen T. Tyman,
> *Ricoeur and the Problem of Evil*

> "I like you Betty."
> Ty Webb

19th Century Victorian Age literary critics would have celebrated Ty Webb as an eccentric, an odd fellow, a gadabout, a dandy and a spiffy gink. In the 21st Century, the term "nutcase" will do.

Despite the calculated vagueness and mental vacuity with which he operates, Ty stands for something even if he doesn't know it. He's a new breed of the old breed, a catalyst for change even as he serves as a vestigial reminder of the rotting Patriarchal order epitomized by Bushwood Country Club. And of yes, such is the sublimity of the film that his very name - Ty - is delightfully revealed by acute scholars as short for "tycoon." And, no, we don't know whence his wealth emanates. We don't even know where he keeps his lumberyards.

Magnified by Reinhardt's Class Coefficient, we see Ty abandon his upper-class peers and embrace Danny Noonan and Al Czervick. And thus, as per mandatory Faber College Thesis Guidelines requiring inclusion of White Privilege Symbologies, this Dissertation proudly examines Ty Webb's Woke Apostasy. As such, he is indeed another singular catalyst for this film.

But we're getting ahead of ourselves and we shouldn't let impatience disrupt the best scenes of our film's life. Therefore, casually grasping our Thesis Methodology, we survey three scenes of Ty's above noted sardonic laconicism.

Scene 1 – The Cooter Preference Test

Ambling down the fairway on a sunny day, Ty and Danny confront existential meaning. Let's listen in…

"Mr. Webb, can I ask you something?"

"Sure thing. Shoot, Timmy."

"Danny.

"When you were my age, did you ever have trouble deciding what you wanted to do with your life?"

"Shuh. No, never had that problem really. Why?"

"Forget it, I didn't think you'd understand."

"Do you take drugs, Danny?"

"Every day."

"So what's the problem?"

"I don't know. Did you ever have to take the Cooter Preference Test when you were a senior in high school?"

"Oh yeah, I took it. They said I should be a firewatcher."

"Huh."

"What are you supposed to be?"

"An underachiever."

Ty chuckles.

"I gotta go to college, I gotta," laments Danny.

"Oh Danny, this isn't Russia. Is this Russia? This isn't Russia, is it?"

"No."

"I didn't think so. Uh, the thing is really, do you wanna go to college?"

"Well, in Nebraska? Besides it costs like eight thousand a year."

"Hold on Danny, I gave you, uh, two fifty yesterday. I can't foot the bill for everything so let's not ask for money."

"It's just my Dad, he can't afford it. I haven't even told him about the scholarship I didn't get. I'm gonna end up working in a lumberyard the rest of my life."

Nonchalantly reflecting on his wealth, Ty replies, "What's wrong with lumber? I own two lumberyards."

"I notice you don't spend much time there."

"I'm not sure where they are."

"Oh Danny, this isn't Russia. Is this Russia?"

Soon, Ty decides that Danny should be offered a chance to transcend and shed his working-class straitjacket. In the dialogue to follow, we climb a summit upon which many of the pivots of this monumental Dissertation stands; indeed, one of the many hetero-normative crisis points of *Caddyshack* scholarship:

"Ahhhhh, I like you Betty."

"That's Danny, sir."

"Danny." Ty pauses, "I'm gonna give you a little advice. There's a force in the universe. That makes things happen." Ty then puts on a blindfold, fumbles several clubs from his bag, takes the 7-iron from Danny, and continues muttering.

"And all you have to do is, get in touch with it. Stop thinking. Let things happen. And Be the Ball."

Ty is quiet for a moment and then whacks the ball across the pond and onto the green, an outstanding shot, proof positive of his mystic center.

He then says, "You try it. Go ahead." Ty then gives the blindfold to Danny, who affixes it to his head and then takes the club.

And now, in dialogue uttered by anyone who has ever set foot on a golf course or in a faculty lounge, comes the famous exchange:

"Just relax," says Ty. "Find your center. Picture the shot, Danny. Picture it. Turn off all the sound," he whispers, "Just let it happen, be the ball...be the ball Danny." The wind sighs and birds twitter peacefully. And then abruptly, "You're not being the ball Danny."

"Well, it's kind of difficult with you talking like that."

"OK, I'm not talking. I've stopped talking. I'm not talking now" and then he mouths silently "Be the ball."

And the inevitable result: Splash, a watery grave. But where did it really land? Ty explains: "In the lumberyard."

A poignant moment between these two giants. We pause solemnly. Because there's nothing more to say and they don't.

Scene II – Carl's Place: Cannonball Coming

In keeping with his penchant for *mysticum whackjobius,* Ty has a delightful rendezvous with Eternity, whose name is Carl Spackler.

It is a scene universally regarded by some of the most astute cinematic historians as the highlight of the movie. Others disagree. It begins with Ty whacking his Titleist into Carl's garage living room.

Let us first exult in the tableau: Carl, the filthy, unshaven, lice-scratching Assistant Greenskeeper and Ty, the wealthy, erudite, polished Bushwoodian. From this unlikely match-up, a bond is soon created, a kinship realized, and yes, a cannonball is forged. Farfetched as hell? Na.

Second, let us also exult in the ensuing dialogue of understanding, warmth, and for us, profound depth. Interrupted from his explosives sculpting seminar, Carl hears the window shatter and is poised with a scythe in the dingy light of his hovel. Here now are their words in their very own words:

"Alright show yourself, you little varmint, if you've got the guts."

Ty emerges from the gloom and mutters "Son of a bitch. Oh hi, Carl. How're you doin'?"

"Oh hi. Ty." Note the near-mystical recognition: Carl calls Ty by his name, "Ty." Not "Mr. Webb" or "Your Excellency, or "Duhh?" And Ty responds, "Carl," not "Mr. Spackler" or "Who are you?"

Ty: "Mind if I play through?"

"Uh sure, go right ahead. What are ya doin', getting' a late night or something?"

"Yeah, loosening up."

"Was that your ball I heard ramblin' through here?"

"Yeah, did you see my ball?"

"Titleist?"

"That's it."

"Yeah, it's right here," he says, pointing to a pastry box containing a half-eaten Basho Danish.

Ty glances around at the squalor. "This your place, Carl?"

"Yeah, whaddaya think?"

"It's---it's really awful..."

"Well, I have a lotta things that are on order, you know, credit trouble... Assistant Greenskeeper...they say that doesn't mean anything until I'm the Head Greenskeeper."

"Oh. Can you give me a ruling on this?"

"Sit down, c'mon, make yourself at home."

"No, no, I don't want to stick to anything."

"Here, I'll take this thing off, it's dirty."

"Nah, don't go to too much trouble, please."

Ever the gracious host, Carl reaches through the filth to hand Ty a bottle of fine vintage. "Here, fire it up."

"With my lips?"

"Yeah, right up, just right back."

"I don't think so, Carl. If I could just borrow a wedge or something and open a curtain or something out there, I can get right through the window."

But Carl is in a reflective mood. "People say, you know, that I'm an idiot or something, because all I do is cut lawns for a living, you know...

"People don't say that about you. As far as you know."

"Well, I'm working on it, you know...so I don't ever have to, you know..." Carl's voice trails off as he imagines the endless possibilities ahead. Then he pivots to a brighter day.

"I'm gonna be Head Greenskeeper, hopefully within six years, that's my schedule. But I'm studying a lot of this stuff, you know, so, you know...like chinch bugs, you know, manganese. A lot of people don't even know what that is..."

"Great, Carl – "

"You know...nitrogen..."

"Can I just open a curtain over there, or a – "

"I invented my own kind of grass, too. Didja know that? Look at this. This is registered - Carl Spackler Bench."

"Oh yeah, yeah, I've felt, felt grass like this before. I've played on this."

"This is a hybrid. This is a cross...uh, Bluegrass...Kentucky Bluegrass and featherbed bench...and northern California sensimilla. Amazing stuff about this is, you can play 36 holes on it in the afternoon and take it home and just get stoned to the bejesues belt that night on this stuff. I got pounds of this stuff. Here... "

"No thank you, I - "

"Let's a have a little bit of this – "

"No I don' t – "

"Look at this. I gotta big Bob Marley joint... try this."

"Carl, I really don't do this that often." Ty modestly backs away from the special offering as Carl remains undaunted.

"But I'm studying a lot of this stuff, you know, so, you know…like chinch bugs, you know, manganese. A lot of people don't even know what that is…"

"You're gonna love this…this is dynamite hash. Watch out for this."

"Well, maybe one drag and then I gotta go…"

As Ty is convulsed in coughs and retching, Carl displays his own intellectual honesty: "It's a little harsh." But he remains the courteous host.

"Here, cannonball it…" thrusting the decanted wine at Ty. "Comin' right back at 'ya." Ty willingly struggles to consume both medications. "Then one more of these, right on top of it. Cannonball coming…cannonball coming…"

The action pauses as the two men imbibe.

But it's back to business with Ty. "Can I have a drop, just a drop for myself?" he asks and proceeds to drop the golf ball over his shoulder onto the Carl Spackler Bench sample.

"That's good," Ty exults.

Carl thoughtfully considers and then decides to formally expand on his concerns.

"Can I say something to you... frank?"

"Ty. Frank."

"You been acting psychotic lately. What the hell? Why?"

"Well, I've been a little under strain, gotta play with Smails tomorrow."

"Smails? The thing with Smails is, if he bothers you, I'll take care of him. What you gotta do to Smails is you cut the hamstring on his leg right on the bottom. He'll never play golf again. Because he goes back, his weight displacement goes back, and he stays there, all the weight is on his right foot and he'll be pushin' everything off to the right. He'll never come through on anything. He'll quit the game."

"That would work and I'm, I'm gonna call you if I need that help."

"But seriously, no b.s. If you ever want to rap or anything or just talk or just get weird with somebody, you know, buddies for life." Carl offers a grimy hand in friendship to cement the bond.

"I'll drop by," says a grateful Ty, gratefully embracing the proffered hand and then re-ciprocating the fellowship. "You drop by my place anytime."

"What's your address over there...you're on Briar right?"

"Briar, uh huh. Two."

"You gotta pool over there?"

"We have a pond in the back, and we have a pool, and a pond. Pond would be good for you...natural spring."

"Oh, the pool or the pond. anything would be good," replies Carl, stretching his aching back. He then immediately and characteris-tically loses his train of thought.

"I tell you what, I'm gonna clean this up."

"You go ahead, everything looks fine to me. Thanks for the dope."

"...all the weight is on his right foot and he'll be pushin' everything off to the right. He'll never come through on anything. He'll quit the game."

Ty swings through off of a tuft of Carl's creation, forever sealing their chemical bond.

Scene III – "Make your future."

A significant amount of scholarly research has been devoted to the final holes Ty plays with the Judge, Dr. Beeper, Al, and later, Danny. The blow-by-blow of the match – on which an ultimate though insignificant $80,000 is wagered - is not our purpose here; our bold thesis refuses to needlessly regurgitate the past work of lesser scholars [see Professor Loser, *Seven-Iron Emasculation*, Holt Rinehart, 1982].

Critical to an understanding of the powerful forces which crescendo through the back nine is the long-ignored but crucial scene at the snack hut (here to be formally identified as the "Snack Hut") following the 9th hole, which features a frank exchange between Ty and Al, memorable for its sad ebbing of hope and the realization that all indeed is lost. Because the fact is, Al Czervik is a lousy golfer.

Sitting at a table in the Hut, erratically penciling in aw-ful scores, Al remarks that he is playing "the worst game of my life." Ty remarks jovially, "Hey, don't put yourself down, Al. You're not, uh…you're not, you're not good, Al. You stink."

We realize, as does Ty, that his defeat in the match is more than just the loss of tens of thousands of dollars, it's the end of his crusade for the Proletariat and worse, victo-ry for his arch nemesis Smails.

And then to paraphrase Ty's own God, Basho, the do-nut hole mysteriously closes. Al is immobilized by a broken arm and Danny steps in. And in one of the most troubling scenes of the film, as the audience and the world bear down on the 18th hole, Ty bears his soul and loses his mind.

"We gotta win this hole," mutters Ty demonically.

"Kind of thought winning wasn't important," Danny says, almost tauntingly. Ty is insistent. "Me winning, isn't. You, you do."

"Great grammar" replies a disgusted Noonan, who is fighting his own demons.

Ty stops him with outstretched club and more profun-dity ensues. "Danny, see your future. Be your future. Make make make, make it, make it. Make your future." And here comes the cringing self-actualization which the pressure cooker spews forth: "I'm a veg, Danny."

"…see your future. Be your future. Make make…
make your future."

The transformation again is complete, for the umpteenth time. No longer a forlorn caddy envisioning distant lumberyards, Danny has manfully stood up to the Judge and now serves as confessor to Ty.

"Take it easy, Ty, will ya?" says Danny almost sorrowfully, taking the blunt instrument out of the duffer' s hands.

Ok ok, we know how it ends.

Briarus Summarius

As this chapter has sublimely illustrated, it's academically lazy to treat Ty as a "nutcase." Moreover, it's superfluous to explore his deep romance with Lacy and the belief he was born to lick her face. The fact is, his gentry radical embrace of Danny and Al brings us to cup's edge of the Inequality Empowerment Theorem, even though his humility itself is striking. Even if he is an ace, recall how he measures himself with other golfers: By height.

Indeed, if not for Carl, Judge Smails, Danny, and Al Czervik, Ty would be the giant of the Shack; instead, he is a giant among giants in the wape of the neck of these woods. Some might call him one of the more complex figures in modern American cinema. To which the great man would humbly respond, thank you very little.

Chapter III

The Bayesian Gambling Reflex and New Capitalist Hegemonies

"The move from a structuralist account in which capital is understood to structure social relations in relatively homologous ways to a view in which power relations are subject to repetition, convergence, and rearticulation... violates the rational, enlightened claims of its hegemonic enunciatory modality."
Professor Judith Butler, University of California, Berkeley *Diacritics Journal*, 2005

"You buy a hat like this and I bet you get a free bowl of soup."
Al Czervick

Thus far we've been playing from the intellectual black tees of *Caddyshack* enunciatory modalities. Now it's time for some pitch n' putt as we focus in on our third subject in this penetrating sociological pilgrimage to the essence of Bushwood Country Club. Yes, I know how hard Faculty

Review Committee Members are having it right now and I want to help. How? Deliverance comes in one name composed of two words: Al Czervik.

Never does a character cut as wide a swath through celluloid hopes and dreams as Al, whose stage name is Rodney Dangerfield. Indeed, Mr. Dangerfield's personality is so overpowering that at the recent Davos Seminar on *Dystopian Front Nine Retrospectives,* panelists referred to Mr. Czervik as "Rodney." The individual as dyad, as such.

His role in *Caddyshack*, as with his unique colleagues filling their unique parts, cannot be overemphasized. Indeed, he is another singular catalyst for this film.

Counterintuitively, he is a buffoonish protagonist, a contrived self-parody. But there's a deeper shallowness. *Ipso obviousoso,* Al has no guile. There is no subterfuge to a man who will calmly shift his backside in a dining room chair and then inquire as to who stepped on that duck. So let's take the tarpaulins off the practice green and ask: Who is Al Czervik? What does Rodney want? What drives this man?

…at the recent Davos Seminar on *Dystopian Front Nine Retrospectives,* panelists referred to Mr. Czervik as "Rodney." The individual as dyad, as such.

There is a large body of critical scholarship focused on the Rodent Intersectionality Deduction. It's absolutely crucial to recall the sputtering McFiddish when confronted with gopher trails by the outraged Judge Smails in the opening scenes: "Aye, sir. I think they're tunneling in from that construction site!" pointing to a distant "Czervik Construction Company" sign. Yes, the gopher ruining Bushwood is a refugee of Al's capitalist hegemonies, pure and simple.

Most important, please allow this bold Thesis to proclaim: The gopher is just a stalking horse for Al, *who himself is flying to burrow, so to speak, into Bushwood Country Club.*

Behind it all, Al serves another purpose. Al is the Marxian foil for Smails in the so-called "Snob vs. Slob" disputation. And ja, he is a perfect foil for Ty in igniting Ty's Freudian Oedipal id-ego relationship with Smails.

And yeah, he is a perfect foil for Danny, whose golfing talents he does not possess. And oh, he is the sensuous foil for Mrs. Smails, exhibited in his lovable lechery. And si, he's also the ethnocentric foil for Tony D'Nunnzio and their implied identical childhoods of toil and despair and hauling 50 pounds of ice up five, six flights of stairs. Al is oh, about a three-quarter foil with Drew Scott, who has introduced him to the club. Al is definitely a one-half foil in Lou Loomis, whom he has bribed to keep things fair on a $40,000 golf game. And *chong*, let's add in a one-quarter foil in Wang, his loyal golfing partner, with whom he has purchased property near the Great Wall, on the right side.

All of which is to say that Al is a foil for virtually everyone in the film. Also, he likes to gamble.

Now, through the lens of contrapuntal storyline dichotomy, let's examine this complex personality, who mounts a vulgarian and ultimately victorious assault on Bushwood. Betting long on our Thesis Methodology, we examine three scenes underlying the central role Al Czervik plays in the film.

Scene I - "Hey Whitey, where's your hat?"

We begin with the auspicious beginning and the dramatic exposition of the "Snob v. Slob" Verticality theme: Al drives into Bushwood in his egalitarian Rolls Royce, accompanied by the irrepressible Wang.

His first lines are creative genius: "Here," he tells the young club valet as he strips bills from his wad, "Park my car, get my bags, and put on some weight." It's a delightful vaudevillian throwback with his old school hijinx nearly stealing this ultra-modern movie.

Walking into the pro shop, he warns, "It's an exclusive club, Wang, so don't tell 'em you're Jewish." Then he says to no one and everyone: "Hey kids, I'm Al Czervik and I'm playing with Drew Scott. This is my friend, Mr. Wang. No offense."

He moves swiftly to the counter. "Hey, set my friend up with the works. The whole schmeer. Clubs, bags, shoes, gloves, shirts, pants. Oh, orange balls, I'll have a box of these, gimme three of those, a box of those naked lady tees, gimme two of those, gimme six of those." At the counter's end is a display with a pork pie fedora. Al delicately observes, "Oh, look at this hat, what a lousy hat. You buy a hat like this and I bet you get a free bowl of soup." He then gazes across the room at the behatted Judge and then adds generously, "Oh, but it looks good on you."

The Gate of History turns on a tiny hinge. The pulse of Meaning is awakened with the faintest stir. The gears of Mankind suddenly seize and turn. All before is crystallized as we now see the battle joined. The Judge and Al have met and the Bushwood turf will never be the same again.

"It's an exclusive club, Wang, so don't tell 'em you're Jewish."

Moments later, we're at the first hole and we meet Lacy as Doctor Beeper leers at her meatballs. Al walks down the slope from the pro shop and there's Gatsby, ever-present martini in hand, Wang and Drew Scott.

As Smails slowly and carefully and slowly takes aim, Rodney inquires, "What are we waiting for, these guys? Hey whitey, where's your hat?" The Judge continues his time-consuming tee-off ritual.

"Let's go, while we're young."

"Do you mind sir, I'm trying to tee off."

"I bet you slice it into the woods a hundred bucks." The Bayesian Reflex is now in, if you'll excuse me, full swing.

"Gambling is illegal at Bushwood, sir, and I never slice." The Judge swings his club and the ball slices into woods "Damn!"

"OK, you can owe me."

"l owe you nothing!" Smails yells back.

We know the tension between the Judge and Smails can only accelerate. Because, yes, satisfaction will be demanded.

Scene II – "A thousand bucks you miss that putt."

The thrust of this fuss is in establishing Al's bonafides as Everyman, or "Slob" – the Anti-Judge. The latter is soon consummated when Al deliberately aims a ball at the Judge's crotch, noting "I should have yelled two."

Now, note the sublimity of the screenwriters as they pair Al with Tony D'Annunzio, creating a rare Jewish-Italian ontological nexus. Neither disappoints.

Lugging Al's custom bag because his "brother" has proven unequal to the task, Tony sets the back down and defiantly comments, "Whatta got in here, rocks?!

Al responds, "Are you kiddin? When I was your age, I would lug 50 pounds of ice up five, six flights of stairs."

"So what?"

"So what?" So let's dance." Al's bag displays a new twist. A stereo blasts platinum gold from a popular rock band called "Journey" and there follows a routine golf course dance party scene. Down the course, the already distraught Judge is rattled again. Personal privacy legalisms and noise pollution statutes are bandied about.

Soon we're on the 4th hole having a draft beer from Al's keg-o-later golf bag. Al pours himself a draught and then notes to Tony and Angie, "Hey, you guys are brothers, right? What is this, a family business or what. You know, they say for Italians, this is skilled labor."

Tony returns the banter. "No, actually I'm a rich millionaire. You see, my doctor told me to get out and carry golf bags a couples times a week."

"You're a funny kid, you know? What time you due back at Boys' Town?"

Al proceeds to display the telescopic putter he received from Albert Einstein. "Nice man. Made a fortune in physics."

On the 8th hole, while his caddies are eating lunch and watching a western on his golf bag television, Rodney gazes at his gopher-producing construction site, visible from the Bushwood links. "Not bad, huh? I'll have two thousand more units in the next two years. Hey, I bet they'd love a shopping mall right here, condos over there. Plenty of parking." He pauses disdainfully and then adds, "I tell you. Country clubs and cemeteries - biggest wasters of prime real estate." Hegemonic platforming, to be sure.

"You're a funny kid, you know? What time you due
back at Boys' Town?"

The viewer is in a cold sweat and nerves are frayed everywhere when suddenly, Smails is on the 18th green in front of the Bushwood Clubhouse with Al's party right behind him. Yet again, the Bayesian Reflex erupts.

"Hey Smails, a thousand bucks you miss that putt!"

From nowhere, crowds gather on the edge of the green as a scoffing Smails growls, "Why of all the nerve!" Glancing at the multitudes, the Judge giggles nervously. And proceeds to miss the putt. And then wheels around and throws his putter. We know the putter is thrown symbolically at Al. But it misses.

The irritation scorecard is way above par between the two; some might label it a dichotomized fission of shared self-actualized loathing. Others might not.

No matter. The Judge is right where Al wants him.

Scene III – "Oh Captain Hook…"
Fast forward on your hand-held 8-track remote and in the blink of an eye, we're suddenly at Bushwood's Fourth of July Gala. Why, there's Al, dining with the Drew Scott assemblage at an upper table stage left from the bandstand. He continues the "Slob" narrative so essential to the Dissertation Abstract. "Hey doll, can you scare up another round for our table," he says showering tips on Maggie while instructing her to tell the cook that the meal "is low-grade dog food. Sheesh, I've had better food at the ballgame, you know? This steak still has marks from where the jockey was hitting it."

He leaves his table after stepping on a duck and confidently performs event reconnaissance, again with non-stop commentary. "Look at that one - last time I saw a mouth like that it had a hook in it."

He then has a pleasant interlude with the Judge.

"Hey waiter, this is for you, alright," as he stuffs cash into the pocket of the Judge's "goffing" jacket. He pauses. "Oh Captain Hook, how about that grand you owe me, huh? Hey forget about it. I'm just kidding, alright."

Al then introduces himself to the rest of the Judge's table, providing a few gallant comments to Mrs. Smails: "This your wife, huh? A lovely lady. Hey baby, you're all right. You must have been something before electricity, huh?" He turns to Bishop Pickering, "Hey Rabbi, nice to see ya," and then greets Spalding. "This your grandson huh? Wonderful boy, nice boy, alright he's a good boy." And then adds matter-of-factly, "Ok, now I know why tigers eat their young."

Al then observes the dance floor. "Whew, the dance of the living dead." He is briefly introduced to Ty in a moment of portent and then wanders over to the bar to cement the Judeo-Italia relationship with D'Nunnzio with clever and poignant dialogue: "Hey Sabu, Can you make a bull shot?" "Can you make a shoe smell?" replies the saucy Latin. "Very funny, you're all right. Whyn'cha get yourself a real haircut, take this, alright," showering Tony with a large tip. Al makes a further observation: "I tell ya, I've never seen dead people smoke before."

> "You're a lotta woman, you know that? Hey, you wanna make 14 dollars the hard way?"

He then turns to his sidekick, Gatsby: "Whaddaya say we bust up this joint, huh?" He turns to the bandleader "Hey Ringo, play something hot, willya?" and throws cash at the rest of the orchestra, which immediately breaks into the beloved "Boogie Wonderland."

But he's not finished with the Smails'. Al cuts in on the couple dancing. "Hey Judge, give someone else a chance, you lucky devil." He squeezes up to a terrified Mrs. Smails and observes, "Hey honey, come here...loosen up willya?

You're a lotta woman, you know that? Hey, you wanna make 14 dollars the hard way?"

"Youuuuu. Youuu…" The Judge is at a breaking point. "You're no gentleman!" "I'm no doorknob either, alright," responds Al. The Judge continues: "I never want to see that man here again!" But he will.

Betcha Summarius

Our examination ends here because further *Czervikian* scholarship is pursued in Chapter 7. I am well aware that Faculty Review Committee Members frown upon textual repetition in order to artificially inflate Thesis word count totals. After all, I wanna be good.

Al Czervick's seminal place in *Caddyshack* may never be fully appreciated. Except here. It's simplistic to make him just the leading "slob" in the "Slobs v. Snobs" metaphoric gopher hole, into which non-credentialed *Caddyshack* scholars fall, few of which ever reappear.

Instead, Al serves as the self-styled interloper, as do his rodents tunneling in from his condo project. He buys off caddy-interloper Danny and charms insider-interloper Ty to win a grudge match over a crummy Snobatorium.

And yet, essential to grasp in the *grand finale* is that Al has not just doubled the bet to $80,000 because he knows that Danny will sink the monumental putt. No, Rodney is betting much more – he is wagering his ethos, his belief system, his very soul.

But then again, gambling is not allowed at Bushwood.

Chapter IV

SPALDING SMAILS

Neo-Generational Paradigms:
Getting Nothing and Liking It

"Indeed dialectical critical realism may be
seen under the youthful aspect of Foucauldian
strategic reversal...of the primordial failing of
western philosophy for generational epistemic
fallacies and their ontic dual..."
Roy Bhaskar, *The Problems of Philosophy and
Their Resolution*, 1994

"Are you going to eat your fat?"
Spalding Smails

Heretofore amateurish and sub-par scholarly work on
the Bushwood solar system has shockingly neglected
to give Spalding Smails his rightful place in this cinematic
galaxy. Frankly, it has been nothing less than gross academic negligence to view him as simply a bit player. With
submission of this top-notch Thesis, the author is scholasti-
cally driving the long ball. Metaphorically speaking, forget
tennis, I'm playing golf today.

As every story must have its villain and every generation its loser cohort, so must every film must have its Spalding. Alas, screenwriters don't want to do it. They feel they owe it to us. As a counterpoint to Grandpa Smails, this detestable boobie provides the youthful Slacker construct to this golf odyssey.

Whether he's cadging abandoned drinks filled with cigarette filters, vomiting into Dr. Beeper's Porsche, or simply picking his nose, Spalding brings an extant evil to the film. To paraphrase the good Judge, to recognize Goodness, you need Badness. And, Spalding, a pudgy, whining, obnoxious jackass, is Badness. In his abhorrent way, Spalding serves as yet another singular catalyst for this film.

Up front, we sense his name is fraught with meaning: Spalding, as in the golf equipment manufacturer (spelled differently, of course).

And yet, he remains an enigma. All we know is that he's "Smails the Third," as Lou Loomis refers to him when assigning caddies to golfers prior to the Judge's first foursome. One mystery solved: Spalding's Dad is Smails the Second.

Most researchers argue that Spalding's central role in the drama revolves around three key scenes, all explored here in depth – "The Yacht Club," "The Snack Hut" and the terrifying end to "Caddies Pool Day." But let us leave the frog's hair and go where no one else has dared; let us dare to declare, allegorically speaking, that we want a cheeseburger. And a hot dog.

> Every film must have its Spalding. Alas,
> screenwriters don't want to do it. They feel they
> owe it to us.

Because let's confront it head on: Spalding represents the disturbing degradation of the generational gene pool. I do not overreach when I assign it the Briggs-Meyer Quantum: Spalding as an easy backhander central to the film's unspoken Danny Noonan/Horatio Alger Modeling.

But no, we're not stopping there: Consider the cunning parallelism in the enormous tension between Spalding and Danny, *mirrored in the symbiotic conflict between the Judge and Al Czervik.* And admittedly, while Spalding's relationship with Judge Smails is a major-league anti-nomic complex, some scholars go wayyy overboard in calling it Euclidean. But not this one.

And no, we're not done with him yet – I guess we're playing for keeps. Spalding, in an eerily Falstaffian foreshadowing, has inserted his corpulent self, and by fiat, yes, the viewer, into the midst of a tortuous morality play, a pungent symbol of the "doodie" frailty of human nature. Disgustedly grasping our Thesis Methodology, we review three scenes highlighting Spalding's seminal role in this film.

Scene I - The Yacht Club: Ahoy polloi
We leave the cramped fairways for the open water and the christening of the Judge's sloop. Like a bad dream, looming

dockside is our slouching, insouciant anti-hero, wearing his customary leer.

Immediately, there is his absurd claim to his assembled colleagues concerning his marijuana: "This is good stuff. I got it from a Negro. You're probably so high already you don't even know it."

While Spalding's relationship with Judge Smails is a major-league anti-nomic complex, some scholars go wayyy overboard in calling it Euclidean. But not this one.

Then when Danny arrives on the scene, Spalding continues his rude commentary:

"Well ahoy, polloi. Where did you come from, a scotch ad?" Recall Danny's terse reply, "Beat it, Spalding." Can anyone say class warfare?

Spalding instantly proceeds to sabotage Danny with Granny Smails:

"My, what a nice-looking young man," she says. "Ah, you're from Bushwood, aren't you?"

"Yes ma'm."

Spalding interjects, "He's not a member, Grandma. He's a caddy."

"Judge Smails invited me at the club," says Danny quickly.

"Well, of course. You're the young man who wants to be in the Senate." Then Grandma gives her Grandson and his wretched female companion a disdainful glance and says, "You two look like a couple of boobies."

It's not over for our skulking protagonist. Later, he is admonished by Grandpa, "Spalding get your foot off the boat!" Mysteries abound only to be solved: We know it was the last foot on the *Flying Wasp* before it was sunk.

Scene II - Snack Hut - Fifty bucks says...

At this juncture, we have witnessed Spalding's vile oaths and chili dips behind a strutting Judge during the latter's second-to-last Bushwood foursome. We arrive midway through that round at the post-9th hole Snack Hut.

Magically, Smails the III appears on the hut's back balcony, deep in thought and soon something else. A crowd of approximately nine spectators including Lou Loomis, Porterhouse, Drew Scott, Gatsby, and assorted caddies are peering through the bushes at a reflective Spalding. In our own writhing agony at this bogey, we become shameless voyeurs even as we try to withstand the impending horror.

A keen Porterhouse offers an observation that overnight becomes a cult classic: "Say, fifty bucks says the Smails kid picks his nose." Spine-chilling, soul-electrifying tension ensues.

He wins the bet.

The very forces of nature require Lou Loomis to double down: "Fifty bucks more says he eats it."

And yes, Lou wins his bet.

Let us pause here at our own intellectual Snack Hut. Let us contemplate the Redemptive Narrative, but only for a moment. Because even with their utter depravity, depraved individuals do exhibit glimpses of grace, like a stopped clock being right twice a day.

> "Say, fifty bucks says the Smails kid picks
> his nose."

Recall that in the final moments of Bushwood's existence, Spalding is serving as caddy for Grandpa. Recall the 18th green, the quiet honor and respect with which Smails the III hands Smails the I the "Billy Baroo." The ceremonial placement of the totem in the Judge's outstretched hands, the murmur of reverence from the spectators. This was indeed Spalding's finest hour. But it only lasted three seconds.

Scene III - "Caddies Pool Day – 1:00 p.m. to 1:15 p.m."

Here is Spalding's finest hour; that is, for academicians who rightfully detest all that he stands for. His appointment with Destiny occurs within the parameters of those precious 15 minutes when the elite open the Bushwood Country Club Swimming Pool to the unwashed.

Like a far-off chimera brought suddenly into abrupt focus, we see the scene: Young people laugh and frolic in the exalted waters, Ms. Underall shows off Olympic diving techniques, and Johann Strauss's *The Blue Danube Waltz* enraptures as the Bushwood Country Club Caddies Synchronized Swimming Team performs maneuvers.

But wait. The keen viewer suddenly senses something amiss. A chocolate candy bar carelessly dropped into the pool by the D'Nunnzio pixie is afloat. As the haunting "Jaws" theme throbs in the background, the danger slowly becomes apparent. Panicked swimmers thrash everywhere and then clamber from the pool and a shocking endgame is about to play out.

But wait. Why, there's Spalding – in flippers, snorkel, goggles, and nose plugs. Why is he in the water during the designated Caddies' Day time period? *Because only he can be the star of the most crude and original swimming pool scene ever written.* Even as he churns slowly toward the object, we, the audience, already know the outcome. And we also know that it cannot be any other way. He deserves this. It is a scene that defines a character, an actor – indeed, a generation – forever.

Only Spalding can bring to a one-word climax the existential meaning of this horrific event, even as his Grandma shrieks at him in terror, she now fully aware of the gruesome outcome of allowing the "hoi polloi" in your swimming pool for even a measly 15 minutes:

"Doodie!" His goggles brush against his loathsome fate; thus is the fate and legacy of Spalding sealed.

Boogerus Summarius
The true genius of this Thesis chapter is that because of revolutionary scholarship and insight, a new thematic

JEFF NELLIGAN

Bushwood nugget has been unearthed. Of course, for your humble author, Spalding Smails was always, textually speaking, a juicy lie.

So now, let's forget about his asthma. Let us proclaim loudly that this once-overlooked and appalling character has been awarded his academic and cinematic due.

Smails the III now assumes his rightful place as a major-minor character in the *Caddyshack* pantheon.

Chapter V

Titular Variables in
Hermeneutic Feminist Marginalization

"...it will here fitfully attend to the putative
traces in Manet's work of *les noms du ère,* a
Lacanian romance of the errant paternal
phallus...a revised Freudian novella of the
inferential dynamic of paternity which anni-
hilates...the phenomenologically irreducible
dyad of the mother and child."
Twelve Views of Manet's 'Bar,' Bradford Collins,
Editor, Princeton Series, 19th Century Art,
Culture, and Society, 1996

"Elihu, will you loofah my stretch marks?"
Mrs. Smails

Thus far our inquiry has fixated on fun-loving misogy-
nistic patriarchy, where character synergies extenuate
to earning fourteen bucks the hard way. Let's now turn our
attention to its opposite: Matriarchal submission.

Certainly, sexual tension is a rare cinematic sociological device, found only in a few works of genius. Like *Caddyshack*. Posited here is a bold, heretofore unexplored sub-thesis focused for the first time ever on the "Belles of Bushwood" who, if I may be so bold, provide us with a boldly rare and delicate interplay of erotic torment.

Let's get right down on these monkey women. Some feminist scholars, most recently from the Womyn's Modality Project, have monologued on the functionally of inter-woven shock elements in which *Caddyshack*, counterintuitively with textual sonography, exalts Sisterhood precisely because of the raw power the womyn wield over the myn. Conversely, the Stuttgart School dismisses the Bushwood *frauleins* as gender non-equivalencies [1.]

The truth lies somewhere lean and mean and not far in between.

Because whatever intellectual bunker one finds oneself in, let's all agree that these three women are central to the drama and yes, as a trio are yet another singular catalyst to this film.

Hence, we examine them briefly and in doing so, thus fulfill the mandatory Faber College Thesis Guidelines on Gender, Equity, and Empowerment. Fondling lovingly our Thesis Methodologies, we begin our inquiry with the trio's unlikeliest ball breaker, who floats in and out of the drama like a witch on a broom ride.

Pookie

First, Mrs. Smails figures prominently because of her presence in four major scenes. Secondarily, she provides the balance of age and droopiness to what is otherwise a film heavily weighted toward two perky young hotties. Thirdly, a co-affluence of the first two.

In reviewing this wizened cougar, let's confess that there is something tantalizing about Mrs. Smails: Her no-nonsense matronly shrillness and yes, her stretch marks.

We first glimpse her accompanying the Judge at the 4th of July Gala, where she is introduced to Al Czervik and becomes the subject of several endearingly obscene remarks. In fact, holistically speaking, it's clear the good lady serves as a sexual toy in this grand cage match between Al and the Judge.

Conversely, the Stuttgart School dismisses the Bushwood *frauleins* as gender non-equivalencies. The truth lies somewhere lean and mean and not far in between.

Second, Mrs. Smails serves as the strident catalyst for the famous "Caddies Pool Day" scene previously noted above, shrieking loudly when coming upon the debauched, watery frolic. She first has the audacity to order everyone out of the pool a full three minutes before the allotted quarter-hour has elapsed. She then orders Anthony "Tony" D'Nunnzio to take his filthy brown hands off of Lacy's shoulders. Then with a Malthusian primal scream, she cries, "I don't want to see another caddy body in this pool!" Last, it is Mrs. Smails who faints when nephew Spalding inexorably surfaces next to the doodie.

Third, it is Mrs. Smails, a.k.a. "Pookie," who at the Yacht Club, commends Danny on his outfit while scolding Spalding and his friend for looking like a "couple of boobies." It is she Danny then offers to escort to the dock as she gives him a beguiling eye (an almost Jungian Precursor for the upcoming bathroom shower scene). Sensing youthful competition, the Judge exclaims, "Hey, you trying to make time with my best girl?" She then ceremoniously breaks off the front end of the Judge's sloop with a champagne bottle moments before said watercraft is sunk by Al's anchor.

Fourth, and seemingly moments later, we see a randy Granny. While showering, she mistakenly asks a half-naked Danny for a "loofah" of the old stretch marks and gives him an illicit, come-hither smile even as her husband works the business end of a golf club through the bathroom door.

We cannot deny what is in front of us. She is indeed, in the words of one eloquent admirer, "a whole lotta woman."

Maggie O'Hooligan

Top 'o the mornin' Maggie, the Irish Catholic rose, innocent and hardened, calm and hysteric - just don't forget she has a deck of Holy Cards that needs sortin.'

If tragedy is a bellwether of Mrs. Smails appearance anywhere, note the ironic tragedy of the complex Maggie-Danny-Lacy Axis: Danny's relations with Lacy *actually begin* with

Maggie's invitation to him to "'boose" tables at the Gala, and the now prophetic dialogue noted here: "You 'feel the water glass, you replace the buddor, when they drop a fork you give 'em a nudder one."

With Maggie, we are compelled once again to ponder the brilliance of the film's scribes. The contrast cannot be too contrasting: Mags, the working-class peasant slaving for her masters at the local country club and Lacy, the smooth and worldwise vamp forever on holiday. Both are pursuing the same manboy, as Maggie instantly understands when she sees Danny fixated on Lacy at the Gala, placing a pound of unnecessary buddor on her buddor plate.

"She's been plucked more times than the Rose of Tralee," Maggie defiantly tells Danny in the club kitchen after the incident, a Freudian sleight-of-hand foreshadowing a Danny's later post-buddor romp with the Rose.

Contrapuntal insight reveals that Maggie knows Danny better than he knows himself. When she is "laihyte," who is there to be the "good egg" in the immortal words of Lou Loomis? Recall also that Maggie is the last female Danny sees before his confrontation with Judge Smailsin what is now known worldwide as the "Fresca Gambit."

Yes, many scholars personally admire Maggie; she seems somehow fresher than Lacy, even though she has fewer curves and a lot less money.

"You 'feel the water glass, you replace the buddor, when they drop a fork you give 'em a nudder one."

In her last major scene, she is dancing gracefully around the pole on the 18th Green, her Holy Cards having turned up a big Joker. She illuminates and advertises the psychological key to Danny's gestalt when she notes, "Noonan, I knew you'd do the right thing."

And speaking of doing all the wrong things, we arrive at...

Lacy Underall

Critical space theoreticians assign Lacy a C-minus. The reviews are mixed: A shallow "Madonna with meatballs" in the words of one admirer, but nonetheless a cunning and intrepid heartbreaker in keeping with post-Feminist liberation formatives. [2.] She's a sophisticated yet world-weary socialite from "dreary old Manhattan," as Dr. Beeper says while flexing his gloved hands sensuously. [Note: Professor Kameltoe's monograph on Lacy Underall, "*Vamp or Tramp? Coexistent Modalities in Post-Suffragette Spaces*" rides and drives this theme home].

Despite an atavistic focus on her two physical qualities, she manages to maintain a raw physical grip on the myn. With her peculiar brand of menace, guile, and tight shirts, she brings out the humyn side of two very different heroes: Ty and Danny. It's an unusual stylistic maneuver and certainly an artistic gamble but satisfies Hollywood's passion for intellectual diversion and engagement.

Critical space theoreticians assign Lacy a C-minus.
The reviews are mixed: A shallow "Madonna with
meatballs" in the words of one admirer...

Even as Maggie remains a sympathetic figure in most
cinematic analyses, Lacy, once considered a heartless diva,
has in recent years been accorded a measure of empathy
that is quite remarkable. That's because in unveiling another side to our leading myn, she brings a certain *je ne sais qua*
to the principals, of which we shall never know.

Bootycallius Summarius
Once again, a new scholastic – historic, really - break-
through is celebrated with this Thesis in its according the
Belles of Bushwood the chick cred they so richly deserve. It
can no longer be ignored: They maintain an unflinching,
ball-busting power over the leading myn actors – Danny, Ty,
and Judge Smails, and let's don't discount Al's gentlemanly
interest in Pookie.

In so many visible and invisible ways, flitting across the
landscape, camouflaged at times by the brasher egos of the
male stars, the Belles provide an almost angelic quality to
the prism of the film, bringing a measure of compassion,
love, and saliva lines to the harsh reality of life at Bushwood.

Footnotes

1. *"Golferinnen große brüste und gut frauen Aussehende"* Professor Dieter, et. al.; Dresden University Press, 2016.

2. Please see Professor Breastes' "Feminist Torment and Men's Lounge Marginalization" *Sports Illustrated*, May, 2011.

Chapter VI

The Mob in Ethno-Centric Deviant Theory

"…resuming the ontological indifference of
all minority social identities as defining op-
pressed or dominated groups, a politics in
which differences are sublimated in the con-
stitution of a minority identity…*affirming* the
identities specific to those experiences."
John Guillory, *Cultural Capital: The Problem of
Literary Canon Formation*, 1995

"I ain't payin' fifty cents for no Coke."
Anthony "Tony" D'Nunnzio

One of the countless miracles of *Caddyshack* is its affirma-
tion that we are allowed to revel in crude stereotypes
and rejoice in condescension while happily trodding upon
human sensibilities.

Publius grotesqian, the film does not disappoint in the
cavalcade of characters at whose expense we can laugh derisively and uncontrollably: McFiddish, Porterhouse, the
D'Nunnzios, Wang, Lou Loomis, Motormouth, Gatsby,

Drew Scott, Wang, and the lovable Havercamps. Certainly they are bit players, unknowns and often pathetic. But can we imagine this film without them? In their own appalling fashion, they are *en toto,* another singular catalyst for this film.

Thus, in adhering to Faber College Thesis Guidelines on Celebrating Diversity and Inclusion, and, through rigorous yet compassionate contextualization, we will collectively identify these wretches as *Everyone Else.*

In their painful archetypes, they are still human beings, even if they are filthy and crude and easy targets for scorn and derision. Their names, faces, flaws, and their vacant stares all underscore that one of the unheralded threads in *Caddyshack* is to bring the humynkinds of the world together, making for a tempestuous and toxic ethno-socio bouillabaisse. Certainly it is wrong – think *Badness* - to casually snub the less privileged of our society. But at Bushwood, it's done with gusto.

Publius grotesqian, the film does not disappoint in the cavalcade of characters at whose expense we can laugh derisively and uncontrollably.

From the first scenes of the Noonan Catholic family pathos and the befuddled, unkempt Scot, McFiddish, we know this tableau is gonna be gravy. Immediately in the film we rejoice in good-natured hilarity at the expense of others. "Hey Fred," says the Judge in the men's locker room, "Did you hear the one about the Jew, the Catholic, and the colored boy?" We learn that Fred is an Episcopal Bishop and that within earshot is Porterhouse, the loyal and African-American clubhouse functionary.

Even in cameos, these genuine inferiors play a key role. Indeed, take Porterhouse and his looming presence in three opening scenes. First, like some kind of house servant, he is angrily summoned and ordered to call a tow truck because some hapless Bushwoodian has parked a brown Audi in the Judge's space. He's the patronized victim of the aforementioned "colored boy" joke. Then the loyal manservant is chastised for wax buildup on the Judge's golf shoes and sternly ordered to "strip, wax, and apply cream to them with a fine shammy." And yes, they're wanted "chop chop!" Porterhouse responds to the challenge with enthusiasm, buffing the golf shoes in a shower of sparks that proves his devotion. All in all, a solid performance turned in by the film's token African American.

Beyond the overt racism, consider as well the film's Continental troupe. D'Nunnzio is right out of central casting - the cool, tough, chain-smoking Latin, insouciantly tossing his black locks as well as several winning one liners: "Ohh, Madonna with meatballs': "Can you make a shoe smell?"; and, always the classic, "Mr. Havercamp, your ball's right over there."

Note as well, Tony's brother, Angie, at the point of a pitchfork with Carl; androgynous little Joey, struggling mightily with the Al's custom keg-o-later-phone-stereo-television golf bag and later, the doodie originator. [1. and 2.]

Moving geographically north by northwest, we come to the Scot, Sandy McFiddish, Bushwood's head greenskeeper and yet another welcome and buffoonish caricature: Red-nosed, bearded, and always clutching a grubby tam-o-shanter. He has several more lines than Wang, four of which remain minor classics: "'Eee'll put me best 'mon on it!" "'Deemit mon, I told you to cut the long grass on the thirteenth-hole and mow the practice green!" "No more slacking off!" And finally, the beloved, "I want you to 'keeeel ever' golfpher on the course."

Porterhouse responds to the challenge with enthusiasm, buffing the golf shoes in a shower of sparks that proves his devotion.

In many ways, the martini-swilling Gatsby is the unsung hero. He's a minor player in every major scene: Playing cards ("Do you have any...eights?") when the Judge enters the Club for the first time; greeting Al and Wang at the first tee; yukking it up with Al at the Fourth of July gala; shooting pool during the penultimate Smails/Czervik Confrontation in the lounge; and, a high-stakes player during the surreptitious wagering on Spalding's horror. And who can forget Drew Scott, who introduces Al to the Bushwood fold? I can't. [3.]

Though a thoroughly undeveloped character who utters not a single word of dialogue, Wang serves his purpose well as a cruelly drawn, bespectacled Chinese cartoon fig-

60

ure who theatrically takes the edge off Al in the opening scene. Note that after the first 18, Wang is never seen again and it's doubtful he was Jewish.

There's that cut-up, Motormouth, nearly a subjunctive catalyst to fellow caddy Danny, but not. He appears in four crucial scenes: He smugly relates the tragic tale of Carl Lippbuam; good-naturedly mocks Danny while speaking to a driver, "I always wanted to be a golf club"; is an unwelcome caddy for Ty during the back nine of destiny - "Don't smile at me a lot, ok?"; and, who can forget his spread-eagled airborne plunge into the pool on Caddies Day wearing a bag of golf clubs? I know I won't.

Last, consider Lou Loomis. So what if he has a severe gambling problem, he also has a cleanliness fetish as well: "You, Angie, pick up that blood." Pick it up, indeed.

And he does have a sense of decorum: Recall the trenchant soliloquy:

"I'm gonna put it right on the line. There've been a lot of complaints lately. Fooling around on the course...bad language...smoking grass...poor caddying. If you guys wanna get fired, be replaced by golf carts, just keep it up." Of course, the threat is hollow; one cannot imagine the film without caddies.

There is his status as referee before the final 18 holes of Bushwood's existence. Al quietly thrusts cash into his hand, admonishing him, "Hey tiger, keep it fair, keep it fair."

"No, I can't accept," says Lou, dedication and honesty illuminated as he begins counting the bribe.

Most critical is a key fact revealed for the first ever here in these pages. I think. Lou Loomis plays a little-known and yet pivotal role in the movie when he answers the phone at the caddyshack with the greeting, "Caddyshack." It is the only time that word, yes, is mentioned in the entire film of that name.

Other objects of our derision include Terry the Hippy, the longhaired, drug peddling, counterculture man-child hanging out at the local yacht club. Then there are the hapless and befuddled Havercamps, symbolic of true aristocratic rot, appearing in three key scenes: Staggering around the course with D'Nunnzio as their caddy; propped up at the Fourth of July gala; and, tottering visitors on the landing of the Smails' mansion when the tea set comes crashing down from the second floor during the Judge's raged pursuit of Danny, sparking the oft-quoted line from Mrs. Havercamp, "That must be the tea."

Al quietly thrusts cash into his hand, admonishing him, "Hey tiger, keep it fair, keep it fair."
"No, I can't accept," says Lou, dedication and honesty illuminated as he begins counting the bribe.

The real low-brow homecoming for all, though, is the post-9th-hole Snack Hut scene. The club regulars and caddies have surreptitiously been following the action, flitting from tree to bush like petty thieves. What a horrifically fabulous panorama; a film curtain call, so to speak. Only no. There they are again during Danny's final putt.

Lowbrowius Summarius

Fundamentally, this rich peasant casserole seasoned with ethnic spice and low socio-economic sauce simmers along rather pleasantly. Note that each character plays easily into a self-parody that is as transparent as it is believable. Each one is an exquisite caricature in his or her own right.

More important, in a truly guttural sense, the unfortunates comprising Everyone Else are a collective silhouette, casting a shadow against a monolith, if you will, called Bushwood. Bit players, yes, but the world needs ditch diggers, too.

Footnotes

1. Please see the Yale Seminars featuring Dr. Kohl-Slaw's paper on *"Newtonian Atomism in the D'Nunnzio Family Centrality."* New Haven, 2006.

2. Despite the centuries-old Irish and Italian conflict, note that D'Nunnzio at the end is seen running up the fairway with a victorious Danny, proving we are all brothers under the skin. Within the lower classes, of course.

3. Personal footnote: As the catalyst for Al, Drew Scott retains a special place in the author's scholarly heart.

Chapter VII

Proto-Authoritarian Totems and The Billy Baroo

"...marked a shift from a form of Althusserian theory that takes structural totalities as theoretical objects...a renewed conception of hegemony as bound up with the strategies of the rearticulation of authoritarian power."
Further Reflections on Conversations of Our Time,
Judith Butler Diacritics, Volume 27, Number 1,
Spring 1997

"Spalding get your foot off the boat!"
Judge Smails

The panoramic landscape of the allegoric 36-hole American Stage is marked by millions of small but insignificant actors and actresses. Conversely, there are only a few giants. Anthropologically speaking, these celluloid mastodons roam the screens of our universe, blaring loud and whispering softly, effortlessly exuding confidence, guile, artistic presence, legal bearing, unbridled arrogance, and they never slice. That would be Judge Elihu Smails.

In the 21st Century, perhaps because his grips are worn, he is the film's most difficult character to grasp intellectually. That is, until this Thesis Voyage takes us into what those of us wise in academic backspin call "the next penultimate chapter."

Most duffers, even scratch players find a North Star in Judge Smails. Or as he is sometimes and irreverently known, Smails. Whatever his handle, the mere mention of his name strikes like a thunderclap, bringing to mind a thousand images, resounding and echoing off the fairways of our minds. Why, *checkitoutius:* Consider the title itself – "Judge" - as in judger of all *vis a vis* the Dean Wermer Theorem.

To many devotees and sheer fanatics, the good Judge has come to symbolize *Caddyshack* in all its sound and fury. For example, here's one of his many monumental contributions to the movie: *Every one of the characters in the film utters the Smails' name.* [1.]

He is an overarching presence, a villain and a tempter. Proto-authoritarian tyrant, yes, but also a Pookie-loving windbag. Why, he built Bushwood. In his own way, he is a singular catalyst for this film.

Titan as he is and titan as he lives, our Judge is enmeshed in four major battles, a Quad-Front war, if you will: With the gopher, with Al, with Ty, and last, with Danny.

In the 20th Century, perhaps because his grips are worn, he is the film's most difficult character to grasp intellectually.

Unbelievably, as if the sheer stamina of this giant can be comprehended, in addition to the titanic struggles with the film's leading characters, the good Judge is enmeshed in a metaphoric four jack with cast members McFiddish, Spalding, Porterhouse, and Lacy. It's frankly more than one man, however strong, can handle. But let us recall: He's no slouch himself.

Hence, Faculty Review Committee Members, I present you with this research gem: The besieged, the courageous, the misunderstood Judge Smails, in the grand tradition of drama fulfills all of the roles of the quintessential Byronic Anti-Hero.

Yes, because through some twisted perversion of values and accident of Fate, Judge Smails is turned into an ugly caricature and Al made to look like an innocent, even during the appalling duck-sitting episode. Although not the purpose of this Dissertation, this twist in perceived Judeo-Christian dichotomies has chilling implications (which I hope to explore in an upcoming *Socio-Jive* journal article with a research grant from the Faber College Humanities Department, but only if this baby gets Thesis Accreditation).

Hence, stickumed tightly to the Thesis Methodology, here are four scenes that underscore the formative character slices of Judge Smails.

Scene I - Gophers & Golf Courses

Our introduction to the good Judge exemplifies the condition in which we find him many times throughout the film: Total and complete sputtering outrage. The opening scene of' his confrontation with the gopher underlies so much of this Thesis thrust that I will hammer you with it again:

The gopher *actually symbolizes Al Czervik*. Both the gopher and Al are villains, surreptitiously tunneling in and threatening Bushwood and its way of life. Leaping from his Rolls Royce in the opening scene, Smails yells for Bushwood's ruddy Head Greenskeeper. It is recounted in print for the first time ever here in this Thesis:

"McFiddish!! Do you know what I just saw?"

"No sir!"

"A gopher!"

"Gopher! Where?!" McFiddish says in wild desperation as he twists a soiled tam-o-shanter nervously in his hands.

"Do you know what gophers can do to a golf course?!" Smails says testily. As that old Greek linksman Aristotle once said, "Those who wish to succeed must ask the right preliminary questions."[2.]

The opening scene of' his confrontation with the gopher underlies so much of this Thesis thrust that I will hammer you with it again: The gopher *actually symbolizes Al Czervik*.

"Aye, sir. I think they're tunneling in from that construction site over yonder," says a jangled McFiddish, pointing to a sign proclaiming "Czervik Construction Company."

The symbolic juxtaposition cannot be lost on any serious viewer, or child.

We now know that the gopher and Al are Prophets of Doom befalling Bushwood. With his glance at the 14th green flag being dragged down into the hole by the gopher, Smails turns in a single moment from a man totally in control of his own destiny to a man in a losing fight for survival.

But there's more. In his naiveté regarding the cosmic plans ahead for himself, the Judge gestures angrily at the site and spits out, "Czervik, huh. Well, I'll slap an injunction on them so fast it'll make their heads spin! And youuuu" he adds grimly to the hapless McFiddish, "You better get rid of those gophers. Or I'll be looking for a new Greens-keeper. Is that clear?"

"Aye sir! Very clear sir! Eee'll put me best man 'oine it!"

Lightening quick, Carl is introduced and the stage set for Bushwood's eventual Armageddon. In the blink of an eye, the sharp-eyed Judge has unwittingly unleashed the forces of Cataclysm.

Scene II - Wax Buildup & Stickum

With barely time to breathe, we move on. Immediately capturing the tension and tartness of the screenplay is the rapid-fire sequence inside the Bushwood Country Club Men's Locker Room. In a scant 42 seconds, Smails orders Porterhouse to call a tow truck because there's a brown Audi parked in his space, jovially tells a racist joke to the good Bishop, buttonholes Ty about his golf score, shouts at Spaulding, and then displays his thundercloud anger. Wielding his golf shoes in hand, he bellows: "Oh Porter-

house! Look at the wax buildup on these shoes! I want
that wax stripped off there, then I want them creamed and
buffed with a fine shammy and I want them right now!
Chop chop!"

The action is fast-paced, the dialogue crisp, the characters sharp as a tee point. And there is no break in this
pell-mell rush. We move swiftly to the golf shop scene, the
seminal run-in with Al Czervik and the psychic foreplay
over The Hat.

Then, let's skip past a $1,000 wager and the aftermath
of the second known instance of gambling at Bushwood.

"I did not throw the..." the Judge is explaining to a club
patron, whose wife lies prone as Dr. Beeper nuzzles her
breasts, pretending to listen for a heartbeat.

"Well, if you didn't throw it, how the hell did it get
here?!" yells the man. A club aide rushes up, "What seems
to be the problem?"

"He almost killed my wife with his damn club!"

"It slipped!" pleads the Judge.

"Slipped!" yells the patron disgustedly.

"It was an accident. It slipped out of my hands."

Here comes the pivot. Instinctively seizing an oppor-
tunity for self-betterment, Danny steps in and moves closer to the Judge and...wait for it...*symbolically moves closer to
the Judge.*

"I noticed your grips were worn, sir. I should have it mentioned it to you before. I, I can put some stickum on there
for you. It's all my fault."

The Judge immediately sees his opening. "Good! It's a
good idea! Next time be more careful!" he shouts at Danny.

Turning to the adults, he mutters, "Kids…what are you gonna do?"

He offers to pay for their disrupted lunch and then says to Danny, "Danny, see you at the table, uhh, sign your card."

"There are more important things than grades. Winning the caddy tournament, for instance."

Moments later: "Thanks for helping me back there," says the Judge, eyeing Danny conspiratorially. "You're a good caddy. Something to be very proud of." He pauses. "Hey, do you know we're giving another caddy scholarship this year?"

"Uh, yes, I heard something about that sir, but my grades in high school weren't actually that outstanding."

"There are more important things than grades. Winning the caddy tournament, for instance. Might look pretty good on a young fella's application."

He then informs Danny he's gunning for Ty Webb, hands over a measly tip, and struts off. The first round in this psycho-transformative morality play is over. The Judge has brought Danny to the Dark Side.

Scene III – "Buy Bushwood?!"

Just 39 hours later, we find ourselves in the Bushwood Country Club Men's Lounge. There are harsh words for the tipsy, apostate Bishop, chastened by God on the 9th hole. And now the now-famous confrontation with Al, who comes into the Men's Lounge with a striking blond Woman and says, "Hey boys, how are ya. Hey, we're both starving, when do we eat?"

An enraged Judge can take it no longer and strides across the room.

"You...YOU! You have worn out your welcome at Bushwood, sir!"

Non-plussed because he's wholly in his dialectic, Al replies, "Well is that so. Who made you pope of this dump?"

"Bushwood, a dump!! Well, I'll guarantee you'll never be a member here."

"Are you kidding? You think I'd join this crummy snobatorium? Why this whole place sucks."

"Su-su-su-su--"

"That's right, sucks. Only reason I'm here is maybe I'll buy it."

"Bu-bu-bu-bu-buy Bushwood!? You!" He then proceeds to strangle Al.

After Ty releases Dr. Beeper from a headlock, cooler heads intervene and we soon retire to the Judge's office where he demands satisfaction, and alas, gets none.

We've survived a mind-boggling string of episodes: The Bishop embraces Nietzsche, Bushwood is slandered, the Judge commits bodily assault, Ty abandons the Judge. The *Flying Wasp* sits in a watery grave. It's all as rich as caviar where the fisherman was hitting it. Penultimate or ultimate, whatever, it's more angst and sheer provocation than any man can bear. It is nothing less than the Judge against the World.

""Are you kidding? You think I'd join this crummy snobatorium? Why this whole place sucks."

With Al, the conflict began subliminally through the pesky rodent has now evolved into all out total war. With Ty, the battle is joined as layers of distaste and lies about his Dad are peeled away at last. With Danny, it is an association based on guile and hypocrisy, the Judge wanting to bring Danny away from "badness" only to introduce him to it.

Those of us wise in the ways of Hollywood's phantasms know that despite their golf skills and despite Al's incompetence, Smails and Dr. Beeper will lose the match. But do we know that the whole of Bushwood will be lost as well?

Scene IV – The Billy Baroo

Let's place Basho, the Lama, and Atheism aside for the moment – because it is with his final putt at Bushwood Country Club that Judge summons his own God.

Hear even now those magic words: "Spalding, this calls for the ole Billy Baroo." Spalding the III removes the Totemistic icon from the Judge's bag. The Judge lovingly removes the scarlet cover from the symbolic sword and softly speaks to it, as though it were alive. Again, count on your insightful author to spot the psychological minutiae: This is where we finally see the Judge as a human being with feelings, even if they are directed at an inanimate object.

His prayers commence: "Ohhhhhhh, Billy Billy Billy Billy Billy Billy. Ohhhh. Billy Billy, Billy. This is a big one, Billy. Forty thousand dollars, Billy," he gasps.

Let's face it: This looming putt is in no way a symbolic knee-knocker dreamed up by some pretentious, gibberish-spouting academic. This is the real thing. And he sinks it.

Fresca Summarius
Despite the ball's victory lap, there will alas, be no victory lap for our brave Bushwood Magistrate. Because moments later, all is lost.

To reiterate for those who haven't been paying attention, the Judge is the dialectical convergence of the whole film – the Marxian struggle with Danny, the "Slob v. Snob" Manichean dichotomized fission with Al and the Oedipal wrangle with Ty.

"Ohhhh. Billy Billy, Billy. This is a big one, Billy. Forty thousand dollars, Billy,"

Yes, he is a most divisive duffer and why, the hat does look good on him. But the Forces against Judge Smails are too great. It's as if the screenwriters actually planned it this way. For him, the man worthwhile is the man who can smile when his shorts are too tight in the seat. But they are too tight now.

Throughout the Bushwood Space-Time Continuum, it's always been winter rules for this cinematic leviathan. But in just a few moments, the good Judge is about to learn what gophers can do to a golf course.

Footnotes

1. This is not the case with Danny's name, a fact which surprises many film scholars inasmuch as he is the theoretical star of the film. For instance, Carl never says Danny's name. Astonishingly, Lacy never utters Danny's name despite their abiding intimacy. Let's go further and embrace the ingenuity of the screenwriters: Does Al Czervik ever speak to Carl? A resounding no. Does Spalding ever speak to Carl? Nope. Does Ty speak to Maggie? Nyet. Does Carl speak to Danny? Nada. Does Ty speak to Spalding? Uh uh. Mrs. Smails speak to Porterhouse? Naw. Does Wang speak to anyone? We could go on and on. But we won't.

2. Aristotle, Metaphysics, II, (III.).

Chapter VIII

Pre-Hobbesian Realism: The Himalayan Fantasia

"Total presence breaks on the univocal predi-
cation of the exterior absolute...which the
reality so predicated is not the reality...the
identity of which is not outside the absolute
identity of the outside...."
D. G. Leahy, *Foundation: Matter the Body Itself,*
1995

"Big hitter the Lama. Long."
Carl Spackler

Sometimes in the course of human events there are individuals who out-finesse themselves.

They fit within no Methodological framework. Except
this one. And I know that along with Faculty Review Committee Members, there are tears in our eyes as I line up
this last chapter.

Although he is only the Assistant Greenskeeper, it is
universally accepted that Carl Spackler is the sole depar-
ture point for any rigorous intellectual dialogue on *Cad-*

dyshack. His Himalayan stature reveals a complexity rarely glimpsed in modern cinema, just as his Hobbesian madness spells doom for a Bushwood CC ultimately devoured by fire and flame. Indeed, he may be the most singular of all the singular catalysts of this film.

Carl's delusion spans philosophy's 18 Holes, a doctor's orders of Hinduism, Freudianism, Wagnerianism, and I will coin a phrase here, doubtless to enter all future literary criticism: Bushwoodism. I would have noted it earlier but I was unavoidably detained.

And I know that along with Faculty Review
Committee Members, there are tears in our eyes
as I line up this last chapter.

In coming to terms with this giant, superior intelligence and superior firepower are required and while other, perhaps weaker academicians might flinch from so daunting a task, not me. Finally, choking up on the Thesis Methodology, we examine the four scenes that define forever this cinematic Cinderella.

Scene I - Cinematic Cinderella

Given the rich texture of Carl's psychosis and insight into Man, we're going to go out on an academic limb and combine two remarkable scenes into one scene. Also, because they occur one right after the other.

Carl's genius is to not allow his inner demons to remain inner. And it is here we expound upon one of the classic moments not only of film, but upon one of the most oft repeated soliloquies ever muttered. It's a descent into either truth or fiction or both. I speak, of course, of the spellbinding monologue, repeated worldwide in a thousand tongues, echoing throughout the mansions of cinema. Yes, the "Cinderella Story."

Stage setter: We find Carl outside the clubhouse near the first tee, dressed exquisitely in assistant greenskeeper *de trop chevalier*. He has a weed cutter in one hand and he begins muttering to himself while lining up strokes on a row of mums.

Here it is, for the few individuals alive who don't have it memorized:

> "What an incredible Cinderella story. This unknown, comes outta nowhere to lead the pack at Augusta. He's at the final hole. He's about 455 yards away and he's, ahhh gonna hit about a two-iron, I think. Boy, he got a hold of that. The crowd is standing on its feet here at Augusta, the normally reserved Augusta crowd…going wild…for this young Cinderella who's come out of nowhere. He's got about 350 yards left. He's gonna hit about a five-iron, don't you think? He's got a beautiful backswing that's…oh, he got a hold of that one! He's gotta be pleased with that. The crowd is just on its feet here…uhh,

he's a Cinderella boy, uh, tears in his eyes I guess, as he lines up this last shot. And he's got about 195 yards left, he's got about a, it looks like he's got about an eight-iron. This crowd has gone deathly silent. Cinderella story, outta nowhere, former greenskeeper now about to become the Masters champion. It looks like a mirac...it's in the hole! It's in the hole!"

Shaking our heads in disbelief, exhausted by the artistry and insight, we are denied rest. Because the very stars align in the heavens and suddenly Carl is dragooned into caddying for His Right Honorable Bishop Pickering. The gathering storm has scared off the more timid Bushwood duffers. But not our Holy Man, who in his infinite wisdom mistakes Carl for a caddy and says, "Hey young fella, I was hoping to squeeze in nine holes before this rain starts." Carl says obsequiously, "Uh, certainly your Eminency." Then the Episcopalian Pontif kindly demands, "Take my bag, eh!" to which Carl mumbles, "Uh, certainly your Magnificence." The Highest of High gently adds, "OK, c'mon, chop chop! Let's go!"

The first several holes are played as the heavens begin to roar and the rain streams down in a quasi-Biblical Ten Commandments scene of torment and mayhem. The skies boil even higher and a thirteen-foot putt miraculously is blown into the cup by a Divine Wind.

Even the servile Carl is moved to observe, "Can't believe the way you're hittin' the ball, sir. You're really clubbin' it."

A passing Bushwood official says prophetically, "Nice shot, Bishop. You must've made a deal with the Devil."

Beholding the dark sky through the raging tempest of wind and rain, the Bishop then appeals to his caddy: "Whaddya think, fella?" Carl utters a line of unmatched eloquence: "I'd keep playin'. I don't think the heavy stuffs going to come down for quite a while."

Soon, in defiance of his seminary training, the Bishop asserts that he "is infallible." Then amidst the climaxing downpour, Our Excellency flails at the sky with upraised club, pleading in vile fashion that the "The Good Lord would never disrupt the best game of my life!" Which He answers with angry thunder.

On the climactic the 9th hole with the Club record in the balance, a putt goes awry for our Man of Cloth and he screams at the sky, "Rat Farts!" Yes, He had been pushed too far. A lightning bolt is thrown from heaven, brutally felling our Magnificence. Framed by the flash of additional lightning bolts in an all-too-real Old Testament drama, Carl slinks off to find help for the felled martyr who will later insist there is no God.

> Carl utters a line of unmatched eloquence: "I'd keep playin'. I don't think the heavy stuffs going to come down for quite a while."

With this and other scenes, it's quite clear that Carl represents the true descent of man into anarchy and nihilism, and as the final film scenes show, a genuine Armageddon for Bushwood. He's Hobbesian; indeed, to strain the boundaries of academic realism, Carl is Tommy Hobbes' first Assistant Greenskeeper, if I may be so bold. He just happens to live in the 20th century. In a garage at Bushwood.

Scene II - A little monkey woman
Carl's second unhinged role finds its apogee in Sigmund Freud. Why, what else describes his sexually animalistic exultation in several scenes?

Recall, in his first skirmish with the gopher, he is seen dragging a large watering hose between his legs, the perversity as shocking as it is defiant.

The fever only escalates. I refer, of course, to the infamous "Mrs. Crane" vignettes.

Performing reconnasiance on the 6th tee, Carl follows the play of a comely Bushwood maiden and her posse as he slowly works a conveniently located golf-ball washer into an orgiastic frenzy. What follows is dialogue from a modern-day Marquis de Sade.

"Mrs. Craaaaane, I'm looking at you. You wore green so you could hide, huh huh huhhhhhhh. I don't blame you. You're a tramp! Ooohhhhh, that was a good one. That was right where you wanted it. Oh Mrs. Crane, you're a little monkey woman. You know that? You're a little monkey woman. You're lean, you're mean, and you're not too far between either, I bet. Are you uhhh? Would you like to wrap your spikes around my uhhhhh..."

Sandy McFiddish arrives to stop the madness. "Carl, damn your eyes mon! I told you, today is the day we change the holes. Now, do it, and no more slacking off!" Carl momentarily directs his ire at the good Scot: "I'll slack you off, you fuzzy little foreigner."

Soon he is again viewing the lasses, offering up his manly commentary:

"Man in a boat overboard…ho ho ho. You beast. You savage. C'mon, bark like a dog for me. Bark like a dog! I will teach you the meaning of the word respect…"

"Oh Mrs. Crane, you're a little monkey woman. You know that? You're lean, you're mean, and you're not too far between either, I bet…"

These fevered sexual fantasies are so troubling that this scholar, for one, would like to see more. Let's move on with Carl to Scene III. But first wait up - he's got a salami he's gotta hide.

Scene III – Gunga lagunga

Ever present in any academician's mind, and weighted in balance with his triumph at Augusta, is the poignant scene in which Carl relates at pitchfork's end the tale of caddying for the Dalai Lama (pronounced "LAH-ma). It's a rapid-fire scene, the nuances peeled away like the skins of an eye-tearing onion, revealing the many layers of Carl's personality, his inner makeup and his outer calm. His verifiable insanity.

It's one of the two of the most famous soliloquies in American drama and it takes place outside the caddyshack. Once again, it is related here for the hopeless few who do not have it memorized:

> "So I jump ship in Hong Kong and make my way over to Tibet. And get on as a looper on a course over there in the Himalayas." [1.]

> The caddy, one of the D'Nunnzio clan now taken hostage, nervously replies: "Looper?"

> Carl: "Looper. You know, a caddie. Looper. Jock. So I tell them I'm a pro jock and who do you think they give me? The Dalai. Lama. Himself. The Twelfth Son of the Lama. The flowing robes, the grace, bald....uh, striking."

> Carl continues, "So, I'm on the first tee with him. I give him the driver...he hauls off and whacks one. Big hitter the Lama. Long. [2.] Into this ten thousand-foot crevice right at the base of this glacier. You know what the Lama says?"

> Angie gasps out, "No."

"Gunga galunga…Gunga lagunga. So we finish 18, and he's gonna stiff me!" insists an angry Carl. "And I say, 'Lama, how about a little something, you know, for the effort, you know.' And he says, 'Oh, there won't be any money. But when you die, on your deathbed, you will receive total consciousness.' So I got that going for me. Which is nice."

The mind reels, the soul wanders, we exhale knowing the pitchfork hasn't drawn blood. Many scholars believe the film could have ended right there. What else was there left to say? Plenty.

Scene IV - Varmint Cong

We come finally to one of the many pivots on which the film rotates, like a Kantian kaleidoscope of existential reductivism. Such moments are a recurrent theme throughout the film, a super-glue holding the whole thingie together.

In this Bushwoodian World of turmoil and torment, Carl alone is unchanging, his single-mindedness is unflinching, and his presence mysterious. He's everywhere and yet nowhere. He's like Schrodinger's cat. He has a maniac grip on the seminal scenes of the movie and its ultimate protagonist. And now here, finally, we speak of the gopher.

Carl has his own brand of intellectual honesty and yes, it is harsh. Which means that we must view Carl not only as the Assistant Greenskeeper but as a Crusader, a loyal foot soldier in the Sandy McFiddish Holy Gopher War, which rapidly becomes Carl's own jihad. Just like any other human being in this world without end, amen, Carl has dreams. And schedules. First on his schedule is a single-minded dedication to ridding the course of the dreaded rodent, which some scholars inexplicably believe forms the entire thesis for the movie.

It begins with Head Greenskeeper Sandy McFiddish's Proclamation: "I want you to 'keeel every 'golpher on the course!"

Ever the realist, Carl replies, "Check me if I'm wrong Sandy, but if I kill all the golfers, they're gonna lock me up and throw away the key."

"Gophers, you great git! The little brown furry rodents."

"We can do that."

"Aye!"

"We don't even have to have a reason."

"Do it, mon!"

"Alright, but let's do the same thing but with gophers."

From that moment on, Carl displays a low cunning in a string of skirmishes which are nothing less than striking.

Relying upon the exhaustive research that is a mark of this Dissertation, here are collected here for the first time, in a methodologically precise fashion for all of you Faculty Review Committee Members still with me, the potpourri of key events in Carl's chasing, outwitting, and ultimately losing what becomes, to not sensationalize it or anything, the Apocalypse.

Ever the realist, Carl replies, "Check me if I'm wrong Sandy, but if I kill all the golfers, they're gonna lock me up and throw away the key."

After receiving his marching orders that morning, Carl's assault begins. Soon he is dragging the aforementioned large water hose between his two legs and humming a ditty. Let's listen in: "Great big gobs of greasy grimy gopher guts." He crouches down next to a gopher hole and politely asks, "How about a nice cool drink, varmint." He then rhapsodizes: "Scum, slime, menace to the golfing industry. You are one of lowest members of the food chain and you'll probably be replaced by the rat." He then spies the gopher eight feet away, leaps at him, extends his hand into the hole, has his finger bitten, and then explains himself to himself.

"When I have been pushed…I guess we're playing for keeps. I guess the kidding around is pretty much over, huh? I guess it's just a matter of pumping about fifteen thousand gallons of water down there to teach you a little lesson, is that it? I think it is." And he begins irrigating the gopher tunnels.

Unsuccessful yet undaunted, he pursues a new line of attack. At dusk we find Carl in his workshop home, sitting behind a group of fertilizer bags in the shape of a sandbagged fighting position, the so-called "bunker scene." He is tunelessly humming: "Mnunmrnmmnun…mmmmmmm-mm… mmmmmmmm…Nahhhhhhh!!!" He's caressing a sniper rifle - and justifying the coming hostilities.

"License to kill gophers by the government of the United Nations. Man, free to kill gophers at will. To kill, you must know your enemy, and in this case my enemy is a varmint. And a varmint will never quit. Ever. They're like the Viet Cong. Varmint Cong. So you have to fall back on superior intelligence. And superior firepower." And as he sites the rifle with improvised flashlight scope, he pulls the trigger and observes, "And that's all she wrote."

The stage is then set for his stalking of the gopher later that evening below the tiara of lights that is Bushwood's Fourth of July gala, this time as a beer-carrying infantryman: "Uhhh, pay no attention to that uhh, bush, moving around over there by that tree. It's just a bush. Nothing to even look twice at. Nothing to be alarmed about." He sets up base camp behind a tree, pops the lid on a can of Budweiser and notes, "This looks like it could be gravy."

He sniffs the air and his sixth sense kicks in: "I smell varmint poontang. And the only good varmint poontang is dead varmint poontang. I think." He spots a gopher hole, takes careful aim, lets loose with his blood-curdling battle cry -"Freeze gopher!" - and squeezes off a shot that hits the clubhouse porch and disrupts the innocent courting of Ty and Lacy.

"I guess we're playing for keeps. I guess the kidding around is pretty much over, huh? I guess it's just a matter of pumping about fifteen thousand gallons of water down there to teach you a little lesson, is that it? I think it is."

Not only will a gopher never quit, neither will Carl. Two nights later, we revisit Carl, again in his sandbagged bunker; again, he is undeterred.

"I have to laugh...because I've outfinesed myself. My foe, my enemy, is an animal. And in order to conquer him, I have to think like an animal, and whenever possible, to look like an animal." Carl displays his patented twisted leer and then continues philosophically, "I gotta get inside this dude's pelt and crawl around for a few days." We are suddenly startled to see that he is gently sculpting marvelous woodland miniatures out of C-4 plastic explosive. As he shapes and smooths, he purrs, "Who is the gopher's ally, his friends? The harmless squirrel, the friendly rabbit. I'm gonna use you guys to do my dirty work for me." Then, beginning to shake with an eerie, hysterical laughter, he takes a fire extinguisher and crushes the delightfully sculpted gopher bomb.

It's in his final fire mission in which we see his dementia in full swing.

In the last hours of Bushwood, we see him low crawling to a gopher hole, "Anybody home?" he asks pleasantly. "Uh hello, Mr. Gopher. Yeah, it's me, Mr. Squirrel. Yeah, hi, uh, just the harmless squirrel, not a plastic explosive or anything, nothing to be worried about. I'm just here to make your last hours on earth as peaceful as possible. Yes, don't mind this," he says, affixing the detonation cord to the squirrel's posterior. "This is doctor's orders and so forth."

As he drops the bomblet into the hole, he adds chuckling, "Hey, you don't mind if I just pop in there for a few laughs, eh? Ehhh, that's right. Well, in the words of Jean Paul Sarte, au revoir go-phair." Then he backs up, winding out detonator cord from a large spool.

There is a subtle shift taking place in Carl. He, like everyone else in the film, is slowly being worn down. Think of his many dances of delusion – the Lama, Masters Champion, government of the United Nations, Carl Spackler Bench.

Carl's finale, cleverly camouflaged as the film's finale, is a golf course Armageddon. He carefully adjusts the butterfly screws on his battered detonation box, tunelessly murmuring *The Ballad of the Green Berets* - "Silver Wings, upon their chests..." He then calmly says "Four" before bringing the charging handle down, sending acres of Bushwood up.

Some have posited, most recently Professor Stimpmeter in "*Folklore Ritualism in Golf Course Modulations,*" that Carl is a generational character. I would disagree. He is a multi-generational character.

The symbolism hangs heavy; the Cold War landscape, the smoke spiraling over the churned up earth where golfers once frolicked. It is then we catch sight of a figure, clutching his hat to his head and nervously slinking off, silhouetted against a pale sky and a mushroom cloud of massive destruction. In his fevered maniac mind, Carl has concluded that the only way to save Bushwood was to destroy it.

As far as he knows.

Augustus Summaritorium

In *Ecce Homo,* Sir Robert John Seeley postulates "The Principle at the moment it explains the Rule is superseded by it." While this has nothing to do with this Thesis, it demonstrates the depth of my research on Mr. Spackler.

This is what I did turn up: "Soliloquy" originates from the Late Latin word *sōliloquium, i.e.* talking to oneself. Popularized by William Shakespeare in a series of top-notch plays, soliloquy finds its true zenith and consciousness in Carl Spackler. But it's not just his eloquence, it's his schedule: His pursuit of the gopher *qua* rodent is simply a *deus ex machina* in the much larger Bushwood Jubilee.

Perhaps summation is best grasped by a confluence of images across the misty fairways of our mind's eye:

Carl - looper, a pro jock, a man in a rowboat and a young Cinderella who has come out of nowhere….and who ultimately returns there.

Footnotes

1. Please see *"The Epistemology of 'Looper' and 'Pro-Jock' in Late 20ᵗʰ Century Golf Semantics,"* Professor Bunker, Harvard Philology Review, March, 2012.

2. Of particular note is *Fox News* Host Brett Baier and his June 13, 2016 interview with the Dalai Lama on "Special Report" in which he confirms the Lama is a big hitter.

Chapter IX

Towards a Unifying Theme

"When interpreted from within the ideal
space of the myth-symbol school, Americanist
Masterworks legitimized hegemonic understanding of American history expressively
totalized in the metanarrative that had been
reconstructed out of (or more accurately read
into) these Masterworks."
Cultures of United States Imperialism, Amy Kaplan
& Donald E. Pease, 1993

"There's a subtle perfection in
everything I do."
Ty Webb

"Americanist Masterwork" is an abysmally insufficient
term in any serious intellectual or cultural measure-
ment of *Caddyshack*. "Western Civilizational Masterwork"
is more like it.

And speaking of Masterworks, this Dissertation, in *to-
talius profundius*, has provided us with a wondrous journey

– yes, emotive, celebratory, and for the Faber College Department of Sociology, even academic. As I like to think, it's been an intercultural communicative characterization of critically co-optive criteria, a glimpse at neo-Platonic Back Nine subcultures with which Thesis Review Committee Members will see my future. And make my future.

So let's line up this last hole. In the trenchant words of Lou Loomis, let's lay it on the line:

The movie *Caddyshack* is as much about golf as *Moby Dick* is about fishing. That is its genius. But I want you to know that because of this, you know, you don't have to stop seeing other movies.

We know all about the complex crosscurrents and subplots and meta-sexual buddor that inculcates this film. We know an irresistible force has brought us to this point, something cruel and inevitable, like a movie script. We cringe, we recoil, but yes, like the Judge, we demand satisfaction. Here are three final observations as this Thesis ambles off the 18th green and heads for the 19th Hole Faculty Lounge.

First, it's already been noted, indeed pitifully repeated again and again, that the film drives home expertly the whole socio-economic "Snobs v. Slobs" dialectic. Enough.

Second, there have also been some top-notch socio-psychological chip shots: Danny's redemption; Ty's A-game psychosis; Rodney's gambling; Spalding's wretchedness; Lacy's promiscuity; Maggie's sweet viciousness; the Mob's boorishness; Judge Smails' fatal snobbery; and, Carl's sanity. And yeah, I know what you're thinking - c'mon, while we're young.

Third and thank goodness last, ever-present is the socio-theological *motif*; that while to all appearances a secular film, Caddyshack is not without a deep, multi-theist Zeitgeist. And for God's sake, we won't say it again.

> The movie *Caddyshack* is as much about golf as *Moby Dick* is about fishing. That is its genius. But I want you to know that because of this, you know, you don't have to stop seeing other movies.

In summation - *grandius duffermasterpiecus* - when all is said and done and played, *Caddyshack* is a cinematic cannonball for the Ages. Why?

Because to paraphrase the mysterious vision of Scott Martin, one of the film's most acclaimed scholars and author of *The Book of Caddyshack:* A casual glimpse at eBay will note the appearance of 9,038 items related to *Caddyshack*. *Citizen Kane,* cited by many misguided historians as the greatest movie ever made, ranks only 2,863 items. There you have it.

Moreover, the film is more than just a world-renowned major motion picture. It's a profound tale, laden with import, a storyline for the ages, timeless in its perceptibility, yes, *a cinematic triumph whose message of hope and love will endure forever.* I would have arrived at this earlier but I was unavoidably detained.

Unquestionably, this Dissertation has proven that Caddyshack is the most profound and most quotable movie ever made.

And now, as the crowd goes deathly silent for your Doctoral Candidate - this young, academic Cinderella - let's get back to basics. I am well aware that there are more important things than grades. Not this time.

Hence, I humbly beseech the Faculty Review Committee Members: As you review this ground-breaking Dissertation and deliberate on its rigorous scholarship and uncanny insight - its zest for living - that you wise men are going to grant it Full Departmental Accreditation With Honors. And that you're not going to stiff me.

Because you know that I know that you know that this Thesis, against all academic odds, revealed a metaphoric force in the universe.

Need I say that all you have to do to get in touch with it is stop thinking, let things happen, and yes, Be the Ball.

Thesis Submission

Faber College Department of Sociology
Jeff Nelligan
April 1, 2020

ACKNOWLEDGEMENTS

This Dissertation was undertaken despite the significant skepticism – check that, Sandy – total vehement opposition from professional colleagues who doubted my overall grasp of the recurrent hypothetic-deductive patterns in *Caddyshack*. And also my brainpower.

I was told my Thesis scope was too broad, the methodological territory unnavigable, the subtleties too complex and the complexities too subtle. There they were, all the Skeptics gathered one evening over wine coolers in the Emil Faber Faculty Lounge.

"It'll be an impossible task," one rival told me, summing up the consensus. "It would be better to focus on your Fletch monograph for True Crime Quarterly." Another backstabber didn't pull her punches. "You don't have what it takes to decipher the Judge's Wittgenstein Axiom" she said smugly, taking a drag on her clove cigarette. Deflecting this professional jealousy and condescension, I chuckled and replied defiantly, "Don't worry - 'eel put me best mon on it."

Heroically, as some have called it, I cracked open a Fresca and plunged forward like a seasoned academic looper. I knew it was my responsibility to scale the Himalayas of

American cinema and provide Post-Modern Vision to what had eluded lesser *Caddyshack* scholars for decades.

My prodigious work was so wide that I was necessarily forced to omit scenes of great force: Carl in hazmat gear cleaning the Bushwood pool; Ty and Lacy's rendezvous over on Briar; and sadly, the seminal scene with D'Nunnzio and the Havercamps.

And here, I'd like to thank my Thesis Sponsor, Professor Eric Stratton, who on the very first day I showed up at Faber told me he was damn glad to meet me. Also deserving the highest scholastic praise are Scott Martin, the film's archivist, and Chris Nashawatay, a keen observer of the movie's mysterious genesis.

Then there are my Delta Tau brothers who in between nightly toga parties spent days reviewing the draft manuscript – Tom Flanagin, Aaron Hase, Scott Lanselle, Joe Bukovac, Peter Mason and Eric Pikus. Above all, they constantly reminded me that it wasn't over until I said it was over.

Even with this tremendous support, there were times when I wanted to quit; I toyed with shifting to a Masters' degree on Orwellian mnemonics in *Stripes*. But I simply could not let go of Bushwood.

No sane adult male can.

So I played through the hazards and finished up 18. I now know it was my Destiny – along with the requirements of my nearly revoked Departmental grant – to complete this masterwork against all the naysayers and boobies and academic rivals.

Why? Because I felt I owed it to you.

ABOUT THE AUTHOR

Jeff Nelligan is a public affairs executive in Washington, D.C. He worked for three Members of the U.S. Congress, was twice a Presidential Appointee serving senior Cabinet officials, and operated as an advance man on Congressional, Presidential, and national advocacy campaigns. A 14-year veteran of the U.S. Army Reserve/Army Guard, Nelligan rose to the rank of corporal. He is of Polynesian ancestry (Maori Indian) and is a graduate of Williams College, Georgetown University Law School, the U.S. Army Air Assault School, and the French Army Brevet Commando School. He is the father of three sons; two are U.S. Naval Officers and the third attends West Point.

Made in the USA
Middletown, DE
28 October 2020